"Don't look now, but I think the living room curtain just moved."

"Your momma's spyin' on us?"

"I guarantee it's not my dad pulling back that curtain. He's strictly live and let live."

"So I gathered. He's a great guy. You're lucky."

"I know. But if she's watching out the window, you should probably kiss me."

Oh, yeah, life was good. Badger smiled. "Gee, do I have to?"

"Shut up. You liked the mistletoe kiss. I could tell."

"I loved the mistletoe kiss. I was hopin' you might want to try that again sometime."

"I wouldn't mind." Hayley gazed up at him. "And it would be what Mom's expecting to see."

"Then let's give our audience what they want."

A COWBOY'S CHRISTMAS

THE MCGAVIN BROTHERS

Vicki Lewis Thompson

Ocean Dance Press

A COWBOY'S CHRISTMAS
© 2017 Vicki Lewis Thompson

ISBN: 978-1-946759-32-0

Ocean Dance Press LLC
PO Box 69901
Oro Valley, AZ 85737

Cover art by Kristin Bryant

Visit the author's website at
VickiLewisThompson.com

*Want more cowboys? Check out these other titles by
Vicki Lewis Thompson*

The McGavin Brothers
*A Cowboy's Strength
A Cowboy's Honor
A Cowboy's Return
A Cowboy's Heart
A Cowboy's Courage
A Cowboy's Christmas*

Thunder Mountain Brotherhood
*Midnight Thunder
Thunderstruck
Rolling Like Thunder
A Cowboy Under the Mistletoe
Cowboy All Night
Cowboy After Dark
Cowboy Untamed
Cowboy Unwrapped
In the Cowboy's Arms
Say Yes to the Cowboy
Do You Take This Cowboy?*

Sons of Chance
*Wanted!
Ambushed!
Claimed!
Should've Been a Cowboy
Cowboy Up
Cowboys Like Us
Long Road Home
Lead Me Home
Feels Like Home*

_1_

Five days before Christmas, Badger Calhoun waited for his flight out of Denver International to Bozeman, Montana. He got a kick out of watching the ebb and flow of the holiday crowd in the gate area. After spending ten years in war zones, he treasured the ordinariness of it.

A tall blond in a fur-lined parka stood by the windows. She typed something into her phone before slipping it in her shoulder bag. Then she glanced his way. He smiled. She smiled back.

It wasn't a huge smile, but there was enough friendliness to it that she might be willing to chat until time to board. He didn't take such opportunities for granted anymore. Then a guy in a business suit beat him to it.

Oh, well. He who hesitates and all that. But he kept track of their interaction. As suit-guy made his opening gambit, she crossed her arms and stepped back.

Must have been a lousy line to get that reaction. Clearly the dude couldn't take a hint, though. He moved closer, invading her personal space. She was trapped against the window, out of room. She looked in Badger's direction and sent him a clear message. *Help.*

Hoisting his duffle crammed with Christmas gifts, he headed toward her. "Hey, darlin', I'm so sorry. They were out of Ghirardelli so I didn't get you anything."

"No worries." Her expression relaxed into that gorgeous smile again. "I'll survive." She looked over at suit-guy. "If you'll excuse us."

Pink stained his freshly-shaven cheeks as he moved away. "Sure, sure. I didn't realize…didn't mean to…you weren't wearing a ring, so I…"

"She will be soon." Badger hooked an arm around her waist. Her height made for a nice connection even with the bulky parka in the way. "Come on, you. I struck out on the chocolate but we can still grab a cup of coffee before we take off."

"Sounds great." She snuggled against him as they walked away. "Thank you. What an idiot. Wouldn't take no for an answer. But I didn't want to make a scene when everyone's in such a holly jolly mood."

"Understandable."

"My name's Hayley, by the way."

He glanced down at her. Blue eyes. He was partial to blue. "Pleased to meet you, Miss Hayley. I'm Badger."

"Badger? Like the animal?"

"Yes, ma'am." She smelled good, too. Spicy.

"Did your parents actually name you that?"

"No, ma'am. The guys in my squadron came up with it. It stuck."

"Air Force?"

"Yep."

"Pilot?"

"Does it show?"

"Kinda. There's a certain swagger."

"Does that bother you?"

"Not particularly. The Southern accent softens the effect."

"That's a relief." He paused next to the coffee stand and let go of her so he could pull his wallet out of his back pocket. "What's your pleasure?"

"Oh, you don't have to—"

"I know, but I hate drinkin' alone and I need caffeine to maintain my swagger."

She laughed. "All right. Thank you. I'll take a small latte." Her phone chimed. "Excuse me. I'd better respond to this." She stepped out of line and retrieved her phone.

By the time he approached with her latte and his black coffee, she was finishing up her text. "My mother." She put away her phone. "She's loading up the social calendar and I'm trying to rein her in. Never easy." She murmured her thanks as she took the coffee.

"You're headin' home?"

"I am." She glanced up at him. "Judging from that Southern drawl, I'll take a wild guess you're not."

"No, ma'am. Visitin' an Air Force buddy in Eagles Nest."

"Eagles Nest? That's where my parents live!"

"No kiddin'?"

"My dad's a minister. The church transferred him about...let me think. Wow, they've been in Eagles Nest seven years. It's a small town, so they probably know your friend. Who is it?"

"Ryker McGavin."

"I've heard the name McGavin." She flushed. "Probably from my mother, especially if Ryker's single."

"Wouldn't be Ryker. He's spoken for, although he and April aren't married yet."

"Does he have a brother?"

"Four of them."

She sighed. "That's why I've heard that name. My mother has a dossier on every eligible male within a hundred miles of Eagles Nest."

"So your momma's a matchmaker?"

"She has a black belt in it. Whereas I think that sort of connection should be made organically, not engineered like—wait, did they just call our flight?"

"Don't know. Wasn't payin' attention."

"I think they did. We'd better get down there." She started off at a good clip.

The lady could move. Good thing he'd put a lid on his coffee or he'd be wearing it. "Your momma's trying to marry you off?"

"Yep. Sounds crazy in this day and age, doesn't it? But she's a wedding planner and I swear she started planning my nuptials on the delivery table. When I was five she tried to dress me as a bride for Halloween. I won that battle, though."

"What did you go as?"

"Catwoman."

He grinned. "Nice."

"I loved that costume." She handed her ticket to the woman at the entrance to the jet bridge. "Why put on a frilly white dress when you can wear a black leotard and a *mask*?"

"Beats me." He presented his phone to be scanned before following her down the sloping tunnel to the plane. "Where are you sittin'?"

"Ten-D. You?"

"Eight-C. Not far." But they couldn't continue their conversation two rows apart even if they were both on the aisle.

She must be single, otherwise her momma wouldn't be playing matchmaker. He'd make sure to get her number before she left baggage claim in Bozeman.

* * *

Badger. What a name. Hayley took her seat and exchanged a smile with the dark-haired woman sitting next to the window. The middle seat was vacant but wouldn't stay that way. Flights were usually packed these days and especially so in December.

Her row-mate went back to her book and Hayley gazed up the aisle to Eight-C. Only the back of Badger's head and part of one broad shoulder were visible. His dark blond hair curled ever so slightly. It would be fun to touch. She hoped he'd brought a hat and a heavier jacket than the one he had on. He wasn't dressed for Montana weather.

If a person believed in the hand of Fate, and Hayley sort of did, this meeting with Badger felt predetermined. She'd noticed him in the gate area the moment he'd walked in. He was very good-looking—laughing eyes, strong nose and chin, broad shoulders, narrow hips.

And tall. She'd tried to be open-minded about dating men who were shorter than she was. But the minute Badger had pulled her against his side and they'd fit perfectly, she'd sighed in delight.

And bonus, they both understood non-verbal cues. That first exchange of smiles had been easy to read. *You look nice. Let's talk.* His immediate response when she'd signaled for help had thrilled her to her toes.

Pretending to be his girlfriend to get rid of that clueless jerk had been a fun adventure. She was sorry it was over. The pushy guy was in first class and hadn't looked up when they'd walked by.

Nearly everyone had boarded when the last few passengers straggled in, probably people on standby. A twenty-something woman with red hair shorter than Badgers came down the aisle.

Despite the time of year, she wore a tank top which allowed her to show off her colorful tattoos. Twisting back toward a sulky man behind her, she complained loudly about how much she *hated* middle seats.

Then she stopped beside Hayley. "Take pity on me and scoot over one. I'm claustrophobic."

Hayley looked her in the eye. "Then think of this as behavioral therapy." She stood and moved into the aisle.

"But the middle seat makes me nauseous." She adopted a lost puppy expression. "I'm serious. I might throw up. And when I hurl, it goes *everywhere.*"

The flight attendant came up behind her. "I'll have to ask you to take your assigned seat, please. We're ready to depart."

"But I don't want—"

"I have a solution." Badger appeared behind the flight attendant. "I'll be happy to take your middle seat, ma'am. You can have my aisle seat up yonder."

The young woman turned and lifted her gaze. "Seriously?"

"If it passes muster with the flight attendant."

"Fine with me." The attendant looked relieved. "I'll make a note of it. Just take your seats quickly, please." She murmured her thanks as she scooted past Badger and headed back up to the front of the plane.

Badger swept a hand toward his seat. "Eight-C. It's all yours."

"Epic. Thanks." She edged past and did a little victory dance before taking her seat.

Hayley gazed at him. Considering his white knight tendencies, he wouldn't accept her aisle seat even if she offered. "You do realize you'll be squished."

He laughed. "After shoehornin' myself into a cockpit for ten years I do believe I can handle it." He slid into the seat and buckled up. "At least I'm not gettin' shot at."

"Still." She settled in and refastened her seat belt. "That was a gallant gesture."

"Don't go givin' me too much credit. I saw an opportunity to sit by you. That's more self-servin' than gallant."

"I'm flattered."

"Good." He leaned back in his seat.

He filled the space. His shoulder brushed hers and if he moved his left leg even the slightest bit, their knees would touch, too. He only took half of the armrest, though. Considerate.

She kept her hands in her lap for fear arm to arm contact would blow her circuits. Infatuation was setting in fast. She breathed in the subtle aroma of his pine-scented aftershave. Sure did beat spending ninety minutes sitting next to someone loaded with attitude.

She glanced at him. "Does it feel weird to be a passenger instead of the pilot?"

"Yes, ma'am, it surely does. But flyin' myself from Atlanta made no sense. And my arms would get tired."

She grinned. "Guess so. Is Atlanta home, then?"

"Born and raised."

She started to ask if he'd brought a warmer jacket for his Montana Christmas vacation, but the noise as the plane took off made talking difficult.

Once they were airborne, he shifted in his seat and looked over at her. "When we were gettin' coffee you said something about your momma fillin' up your social calendar. Any chance we could meet for drinks while we're both in town?"

"That would be great." His eyes were a warm brown. This close, she could see little flecks of gold. "But first I need to find out what elaborate matchmaking schemes Mom's cooked up. She's a cagey one. She'll say we're going to lunch with one of her friends and then what do you know? The friend's son discovers he's free for lunch, too. What a coinkidink."

"Sounds like a nightmare."

She liked the way he said it. *Nahtmare.* She'd never met any Southern gentlemen before and had always assumed they'd look like Colonel Sanders. "I go through it every Christmas. It's my longest visit of the year which gives her plenty of room to maneuver."

"But why would she try to hitch you up with some guy from Eagles Nest when you don't live there?"

"That's part of the plan. I'll fall for one of her choices and relocate."

"Wow, that's...outrageous."

"Yeah."

"Have you told her she's barkin' up the wrong tree?"

"I have, but she doesn't hear me. She won't relax until I'm walking down the aisle. And she's convinced I'll never find someone when I'm with senior citizens all the time."

"Are you?"

"Quite a bit. I work in elder care, but I do have a social life. I date. I think she's starting to panic because I've turned thirty."

"Lord-a-mercy, that's getting' up there, all right."

She laughed. "How old are you?"

"Older'n you. Your momma would have a conniption knowin' I'm still runnin' around loose."

"Probably. She and my dad married when she was twenty-two and he was twenty-five. In her mind, those are good ages to be settling down."

"People are gettin' married later these days."

"Intellectually she knows that, but I'm not kidding that she's been anticipating this since I was born. She used to have an envelope stuffed with clippings from various wedding magazines but now she's got it all on her computer."

"I'm surprised you haven't had a showdown."

"Oh, we would have if I lived there. She'd drive me bat shit crazy in no time and I'd blow. But at Christmas, about the time I'm ready to scream, the vacation is over. I fly back to Denver, drink an entire bottle of wine, and I'm good until the next year."

"You could threaten not to come home for Christmas."

"Yeah, well, no, I couldn't do that. She's impossible but she's my mother. I love her. And my dad's a hoot. I don't know how he puts up with her. I figure they must have great sex but who wants to think about their parents having sex?"

"Not me."

"Exactly. Oh, and my baby brother Luke always comes home for Christmas, too. I can't miss that."

"How much of a baby is he?"

She laughed. "Not so much anymore. He's about your size. He's two years younger than me and refuses to believe I used to give him noogies."

"So basically you're sayin' it's worth the stress of your momma's matchmakin' to be home with your family for the holidays."

"It is. I guess. But I swear she's escalating the campaign. It seems worse every year. Or maybe I'm less tolerant."

"I can see how you would be, now that you're thirty and all."

"You know, that could have something to do with it. And each year I have more empathy for the poor guys she drags into this circus. They all act as if they've been ambushed. Which of course they have. She always makes the initial meeting seem like an accident."

"Hm." He leaned back in his seat.

"You probably think I should take a stand, huh? Put an end to this craziness?"

"That's not exactly what I was thinkin'." He chuckled.

"What?"

"I just got this hare-brained idea." He turned his head and gazed at her. "You probably wouldn't go for it."

"Try me."

"What if you showed up with some guy who's swept you off your feet? Wouldn't that bring the bachelor parade to a screechin' halt?"

She stared at him and her heart rate picked up. "Some guy meaning you?"

His brown eyes gleamed. "Yes, ma'am."

"But how would that make sense? You're from Atlanta and I'm from Denver. You're visiting your Air Force buddy, not coming to meet my folks."

"Do you travel for work?"

"Sure. Conferences, mostly."

"Then here's our story. We crossed paths while we were on the road. We bonded over the connection to Eagles Nest. Romance ensued. I've had more free time so I've hopped on flights to visit you. Christmas was the perfect opportunity to break the news because we were both comin' here anyway and you wanted to tell them in person."

She stared at him. "Assuming I'd consider such a thing, have you been out of the Air Force long enough for that story to hold water?"

"I've been back a little more than two months. That should be fine."

"Really? Two months isn't very long."

"Long enough. Especially for a guy who's learned that life is mighty short."

She met his gaze. That last statement had the ring of truth. Logically a soldier would develop a greater respect for the value of time.

His idea was bold. It was daring. She'd have to lie to her parents, but in exchange, she'd be spared awkward social occasions with guys her mom had rounded up.

Instead she'd be required to spend a chunk of her Christmas vacation with Badger, someone she'd already taken a fancy to.

He studied her. "What do you think?"

"This really pushes the envelope for me."

The woman in the window seat looked up from her book. "Don't be a fool. He's gorgeous. Go for it."

Hayley peered at her. "Thank you for your input."

"Don't mention it." She went back to her book.

Badger gazed at her. "Well?"

"I like it."

"Excellent." He grinned, clearly pleased.

"But for starters, I need to know your real name."

"Promise not to laugh."

"I promise."

"Thaddeus Livingston Calhoun the Third."

She swallowed a giggle. "That's a mouthful."

"Which is why I'd surely appreciate it if you'd call me Badger."

"Okay. That's easier to remember, anyway." Nervous excitement made her stomach quiver. "I've never done anything like this before. I hope I can pull it off."

"Sure, you can. It'll be fun. We have just enough time to iron out the details before we land."

2

Badger loved nothing better than a good adventure. Pretending to be Hayley Bennett's special guy for the holidays was shaping up to be an excellent one. Even the logistics were falling into place nicely. She was renting a car for the drive from Bozeman to Eagles Nest so he wouldn't need to deal with her parents until later.

But Ryker would be in baggage claim waiting for him. He and Hayley hadn't completely agreed on how to handle that.

She brought it up again as she walked beside him down the jet bridge to the Bozeman terminal. "I still think you should tell your friend the same story I'm telling my folks. What if he lets something slip?"

"If you knew Ryker, you wouldn't be thinkin' that way, so you'll have to take my word for it. Ryker doesn't let things slip."

"But wouldn't it be better not to take the chance?"

"No, ma'am. Ryker and I've shared some intense experiences. Because of that we can't bullshit each other. He'd see right through me if I tried, so I might as well give it to him straight. I've trusted my life to Cowboy many times. I can trust him with this."

"Cowboy?"

"That was his nickname just like mine was Badger. When you see him, you'll know why."

"But you said he runs a commuter airline."

"Because he loves to fly, just like me. But he grew up on a ranch. Ridin' and ropin' are in his blood. I've seen pictures to prove that fact. I guarantee he'll show up lookin' like he rode in on a horse." He walked with her into the terminal and paused. "Nice airport. I like the beamed ceilings."

"Bozeman does a great job of welcoming travelers to Montana."

"I can surely see that." He glanced out a window. "Lots of snow on those mountains."

"Oh, yeah."

"Which way to baggage claim?"

"Follow me." She set a brisk pace, her shoulder-length hair swinging with each step.

He was more of an ambler, but he lengthened his stride to keep up with her. "I've never seen so many people wearin' parkas and boots."

"I meant to ask if you brought a heavier jacket than what you have on."

"No, ma'am. I'm a Southern boy. It rarely snows in Atlanta, but when it does, the city shuts down. We have no idea what to do with that white stuff. Or how to dress for it."

"Weren't you ever stationed somewhere cold?"

"I was not, which was a blessin'. Flyin' at high altitude was the only time I had to endure the cold. Not sure how I would have handled it if I had been subjected to it on the ground, too."

"You've never gone skiing?"

"I've been on water skis ever since I could walk. Never had the urge to strap on snow skis."

"But didn't you say Ryker wants you to move to Eagles Nest and become a full partner in the business?"

"Yes, ma'am. I didn't say I was committed to doin' it. I've warned him I'm not a fan of ice and snow, but he maintains I'll get used to it."

"Between now and New Year's?"

"Not likely, is it? But I promised ol' Cowboy I'd show up and test the situation, so here I am."

"Well, let me give you a tip. Get yourself a warmer jacket and a hat. Or a jacket with a hood."

"I'll take the hat option. Don't see myself wearing a hoodie."

"Eagles Nest has a great Western wear store."

"Then I'll keep that in mind as an option." He rode behind her down the escalator to baggage claim. "Look for a tall guy built like a tank and wearing a Stetson."

She laughed. "There will be a whole bunch of guys in baggage claim who fit that description."

"Could be, but there's only one Ryker McGavin. He stands out."

She stepped off the escalator and glanced around. "Is that him wearing the black hat?"

"Sure is. Come on over and meet a great pilot and an even better friend." Happiness poured through him at the sight of Ryker striding in his direction with a big ol' grin on his face. He wasn't a brother by blood, but he might as well be. They'd made a connection from day one.

He was so glad to see the guy that he got a little choked up when they embraced. Then he turned and introduced Hayley. "We met on the plane. You probably know her folks."

"I do. Virginia and Warren Bennett. I see the family resemblance." Ryker shook her hand. "I'm not much of a church-goer, but other people have told me your dad makes it a fun experience."

"He does. His high school counselor told him he should either be a minister or a standup comic. He decided to be both."

"That explains his act in the Christmas talent show."

She blinked. "What talent show?"

"It's a new thing. It'll be Saturday night at the Guzzling Grizzly. The proceeds go to local families who need a boost during the holidays." He glanced at Badger. "I signed us up for a juggling act."

"Oh, did you, now?"

"I took a chance you kept it up after I left."

"I did until I came back. I haven't practiced much the past couple of months."

"You'll be fine. I've taught my little brother Cody our routine because we need three people to make it look right. You okay with that?"

"Sure."

Hayley tugged on Ryker's sleeve. "Did you say my dad's doing an act in this talent show?"

Ryker smiled at her. "He sure is. He calls it *Holy Hilarity, Godman*. He showed me his superhero costume, complete with a cape. I guarantee plenty of people in town will come just for his performance."

"Count me as one of them. I've never seen my dad in Spandex."

"I doubt his parishioners have, either." When a beep sounded in the baggage area, he glanced past her. "Looks like the bags have showed up. Need me to snag yours?"

"Thanks, but I'll get it." She headed toward the carousel's conveyor belt.

Ryker glanced at Badger. "Does she need a ride to town? I only brought my truck but maybe we can make it work."

"She's rentin' a car. When she visits her folks, she likes havin' her own transportation."

"Okay, that's good. I was going to have to put her on your lap." He gave Badger a knowing look. "Although you might not have minded that so much."

"I'll explain about that once we get on the road."

"Please do. I can tell something's going on."

Hayley came over pulling a large wheeled suitcase and turned to Badger. "I'll text you when I've figured out the best time for you to show up."

"Okay. Drive safe."

"Sure thing. By the way, will you have transportation?"

"I'll figure it out." Ryker was in his peripheral vision, frowning.

"Let me know if there's a problem. See you soon." She glanced over at Ryker. "Great meeting you."

His frown disappeared and he smiled. "Same here, Hayley. You take care, now."

"Thanks." She made her way toward the car rental area.

Ryker pushed back his hat and stared at Badger. "What the hell?"

"It's a long story." He looked over at the carousel. "There's my bag. We'll talk on the way to the ranch."

"We damn sure will." He followed Badger over to the conveyor belt and waited for him to pull off his black suitcase. "You got a warmer jacket in there?"

"Nope. The sun's shinin'. I'll be fine."

"If you say so." He led the way through a pair of sliding glass doors.

Badger stepped outside and gasped. "Shit, Cowboy! It's freezin' out here!"

Ryker laughed. "Ah, but the sun's shining." He started toward the parking lot.

"What's the temperature?"

"You don't want to know."

"The wind doesn't help." He zipped his jacket. Didn't do much good. "Hayley warned me I'd be cold. Guess I need a sheepskin deal like you're wearin', huh?"

"Might be a good idea. Seeing as how you're going calling tonight. In fact, that sunshine you're counting on will be gone before too long. Days are shorter up here."

"I suppose they would be. Hayley said there's a Western wear store in Eagles Nest. Maybe we need to stop there, pick up a jacket."

Ryker glanced at his loafers and cotton pants. "Are the rest of your clothes like what you have on?"

"Yeah, why?"

"Then you need more than a jacket, flyboy. I'd suggest boots, jeans, a hat, maybe a flannel shirt or two, gloves, and—"

"Okay, I get the picture. We're talkin' a major shopping trip."

"'fraid so. You up for that?"

"Not right now. Maybe tomorrow. I'll tough it out until then."

"If I'd known I would've brought you something of mine. We could detour by my house and grab something."

"Hey, that's too much trouble. I'll manage."

"Nah, you need something." He pulled out his phone and punched a button. "Hey, Cody. Yeah, just picked him up at the airport. Listen, he needs a warm jacket. You got one you could take over to Mom's? Great. Appreciate it."

"Thanks, Cowboy." Badger did his best to keep his teeth from chattering. Damn. He could see his breath.

"No problem." Ryker tucked his phone away. "Don't want you to go hypothermic on me."

"Could I?"

He laughed. "Probably not unless you stayed outside for a prolonged period."

"Like t-ten minutes?"

"Maybe in your case." Ryker glanced at him. "Evidently you weren't kidding about being a pansy-ass Southern boy."

"Nope."

"No worries. I'll have you toughened up in no time."

"How?"

"Well, first thing in the morning, we'll go skinny dipping in the old water hole out at the ranch. We might have to chip away some ice, but—"

"You'd better be kiddin' or I'm headin' back to the terminal."

"Ah, I'm kidding."

"I knew that."

"Never fear." He punched him on the shoulder. "We'll cowboy you up tomorrow and you'll be fine."

"G-good."

"Just so you know, April was ready to buy a hide-a-bed so you could stay with us, but—"

"That would have been c-crazy."

"That's what I told her. You'll be better off at the ranch. You'll get your own room and a decent bed." He stopped beside a badass black truck. "This is it."

"Nice r-ride."

"Thanks. Just wedge your suitcase in there beside the lumber. It should fit fine."

Badger lifted his suitcase and shoved it into a vacant space in the back. Then he climbed into the cab and shut the door. The interior of the truck wasn't a whole lot warmer, but at least he was out of the wind.

Ryker climbed behind the wheel, started the engine and switched on the heater.

Okay. The vent was producing warm air. He could talk without shivering. "Whatcha buildin' with that lumber?"

"My brother Trevor and I are building April a henhouse."

"Yeah?" Henhouses. Lord-a-Mighty. He was in the boonies, for sure.

"I promised her one for Christmas. Her mom has chickens, my mom has chickens, and April has decided she wants chickens, too. She got permission from our landlord to put them in the backyard."

"Do you want chickens?"

"Sure, why not? The ones she gets will lay colored eggs. They're called Easter Eggers."

"Aren't all chicken eggs white?"

"No."

"That's the only color I've seen."

"Stick with me, city boy, and you'll learn all kinds of useful info." He pulled up next to a booth, paid the parking fee and headed out of the lot. "But enough about that. What's the story with Hayley Bennett?"

"Turns out she has the matchmakin' momma from hell and she was facin' another Christmas of dealin' with whatever guys her momma dragged over there. I suggested posin' as her boyfriend and she went for it."

"No, you didn't. You're making this up."

"It's for real. The poor woman was dreadin' her vacation and now she's not. But I'll have to ask you to keep this to yourself."

"Are you seriously going to interfere in the Bennett family dynamics?"

"They're ridiculous dynamics."

"Which is none of your damned business."

"I'm making it my business. You should have seen her expression when she was tellin' me about it. She's at the end of her rope and for all I know this could be the Christmas she goes ballistic. I—"

"I can't believe this. No, wait, I can. It's so typical of you, leaping into a situation without considering how—"

"It'll be fine. The story's foolproof. We've worked it all out and it makes perfect sense. I'll go over there tonight and introduce myself."

"See there? Already a conflict. I was going to ask if you wanted to go with me and April to her hospital Christmas party."

"And I would have loved to, except this came up. Once I present myself at her folks' house tonight, her momma will back off. Problem solved."

"Problem *solved*? Your problems will just be beginning, bozo!"

"How do you figure?"

"You'll be setting yourselves up as a couple. At Christmas, in fact, which complicates the picture even more. Couples do Christmas things together. You and Hayley will be juggling holiday obligations from her family and my family, all the while trying to keep your damned story straight. It's a disaster waiting to happen."

"You always think that. What about the time in Afghanistan?"

"You mean when you almost got yourself killed?"

"But I didn't! I saved the day!"

"Only because you're a damned lucky SOB. Logically you should have been shot down. You shouldn't be alive."

"You can't always go by logic. Sometimes you have to go with your gut. Don't worry. Hayley and I can pull it off."

"And what if you don't? What if one of you screws it up and the whole house of cards comes crashing down?"

"We won't screw it up."

"But what if you do? You'll look bad and she'll look bad. This isn't Atlanta. You'll feed the gossip mill for weeks to come. You'll embarrass her folks. I don't know Virginia very well but Warren's great."

Badger got it, now. "You're afraid I'll embarrass you."

He sighed. "Yeah, that, too, I suppose. Listen, you're making a huge mistake. How about texting her right now and calling it off? She's not there yet. If she sees the text before she gets home, then—"

"I'm not callin' it off, Cowboy. I offered to do this for her and I'm committed."

"I'm sorry to hear that."

"Believe me, it'll all work out for the best."

"I doubt it, but since you'll be telling this big wooly to my mom and the rest of my family, you'd better lay it out for me before we get there."

"Be happy to. Once you realize how foolproof it is, you'll be able to relax."

"Don't count on it."

* * *

Hayley rehearsed her speech all the way to her parents' house. Good thing Luke wouldn't be arriving for a couple of days. That would give her a chance to get more familiar with the story before she had to sell it to her brother. He'd be tougher to fool. Maybe she'd end up confiding in him, after all, but she'd decide that later.

She pulled into the driveway at dusk just as the multicolored Christmas lights strung along the edge of the front porch roof winked on. Two spotlights illuminated the hand-crafted nativity scene nestled in the snow-covered front yard. The Bennett house usually had the prettiest holiday decorations on the block, a labor of love shared by her mom and dad.

They'd wound the posts and railings with pine garlands and positioned a lighted tree on either side of the front door. A giant wreath hung there and battery operated candles glowed in every window. She loved it all, always had. That was why her mother's obsession with finding her a husband was such a pain in the butt. It spoiled Christmas.

But when her mom came running out to greet her, the red parka she'd pulled on unzipped in her haste to get to the car and wrap her arms around her only daughter, Hayley almost lost her nerve. Maybe she should text Badger and tell him to forget the plan. She'd suffer through another season. Drink another bottle of wine when it was over.

Her mom gave her a tight hug and stepped back, her face alight. "I have the *best* news. Anna's son is coming home for the holidays. He's an art dealer and he's doing *very well*. Just called it quits with his girlfriend. We're meeting them for lunch at the Guzzling Grizzly tomorrow. Isn't that fabulous?"

Hayley took a deep breath. Game on. "Mom, I have some exciting news, too. I've met someone."

Her mother's jaw dropped. "Met someone? Do you mean *met someone* in the sense that you two are—"

"Practically engaged? Yes. Yes, we are."

"Oh, heavens! I'm flabbergasted! Why didn't you tell me?"

"It happened so fast and I wanted to break the news in person."

"Of course you did." Her mother grabbed both of her hands and squeezed. Her eyes were moist. "Come inside. We need to tell your father. This is huge, Hayley. *Huge.*"

"I should get my—"

"Later. First we need to inform your father that his baby girl has finally found the love of her life."

3

Badger was sorry that Ryker was upset with the new development, but it couldn't be helped. Ryker was a straight arrow. His reaction was predictable, but when the plan went smoothly and Hayley enjoyed the holiday for a change, Ryker would have to admit it had been a good idea. Maybe even a brilliant one.

Wild Creek Ranch was exactly as he'd imagined. The buildings were set against a backdrop of pines and picturesque snow overlaid everything except the well-tracked dirt area between the house and the barns.

The low-slung ranch house looked as if some giant had been playing with Lincoln Logs. A row of colored lights twinkled along the eaves and the porch railing. An old-fashioned lamppost by the front walkway was decorated with a wreath and a big red bow.

Across the way stood what Ryker said was the original barn, which resembled something out of a kid's book—hip roofed, painted brick red, hayloft above the massive double doors. A second barn had a sleeker profile. Both had lighted wreaths above the double doors. Nice touch.

From inside the truck, the wintery scene was charming. But he'd figured out that a landscape like this meant he'd freeze his ass off because he hadn't taken the weather seriously.

"Oh, right," Ryker said as he pulled in next to a row of parked vehicles. "I forgot the Whine and Cheese Club had a practice tonight."

"The whozit?"

"My mom's four gal pals. Deidre, Christine and Judy were in her graduating class and Aunt Jo used to be a neighbor until she moved into town this past spring."

"Is Aunt Jo the one you were video chattin' about with your mom that time I was there?"

"Yep."

"She's the honorary aunt who didn't end up movin' to New York?"

"Exactly."

"See, I remembered. Aunt Jo's daughter is Mandy and she married Zane in September. I have a mind like a steel trap."

"I sure as hell hope so. You're gonna have to tell your story to these ladies, and it better be the same story you tell from here on out."

"I promise it will be, Cowboy. I've been rehearsin' in my head on the way here."

Ryker sighed. "Then I guess it's show time." He opened his door. "Leave your suitcase for now. We'll bring it in later, after the introductions."

"Sounds good. I'll leave my duffel, too."

"Yeah, that thing sure is packed tight. What's in there?"

"Surprises."

"You brought presents?"

"Of course I brought presents. It's Christmas, isn't it?"

"I know, but how could you possibly figure out what to get?"

"I keep tellin' you I'm a genius."

Ryker chuckled. "Like I said, I hope so."

Cold air barreled in when Badger opened his door. He hurried out of the truck. The quicker he exited, the quicker he'd get inside. If Cody had followed through, there would be a coat in there waiting for him.

Ice crystals crunched under his feet as he followed Ryker over to the walkway. "What are the women practicin' for?"

"The dance they're doing for the talent show. I think Mom said something about *Jingle Bell Rock.*" Ryker mounted the porch steps. "They'll probably wear Santa suits."

Badger was right on his heels. "That's not *Jingle Bell Rock* they're playin' in there."

"No, sounds like rap."

"It is rap. That's Sweet Tee's *Let the Jingle Bells Rock.*" He moved in time to it as he crossed the porch. Anything to stay warm.

"They must be messing around. They wouldn't do a rap song." Ryker used the boot scraper by the door.

"That's ingenious."

"What is?"

"The gizmo to clean off your shoes." He used it, too, as he twitched to the music.

"What the hell are you doing?"

"Cleanin' off my shoes."

"No, the jerking around part."

"It's hip hop. That music brings back memories."

"You can dance that stuff?"

"Sure. Can't you?"

"Never had the slightest desire."

"Then you missed out, Cowboy. Can we go in now before my nuts freeze and fall off?"

"Yeah, sorry. I got distracted watching you having a spastic fit." He opened the door and gestured for Badger to go in.

He didn't have to be asked twice. He stepped into heaven. A fire blazed on the hearth and delicious aromas wafted from the kitchen. Directly in front of him in a space cleared of furniture, five women danced to *Let the Jingle Bells Rock.* They looked mighty fine doing it, too.

An attractive woman with dark hair and Ryker's blue eyes smiled and waved as she kept moving to the beat. "Hi, Badger!"

He waved back. "Great job, y'all!"

"Thanks!" called a short, plump redhead. She was likely the instigator. She had some moves.

"I can't believe what I'm seeing," Ryker muttered.

"I think it's cool. They're good."

"How can you tell?"

"Haven't you ever seen hip hop?"

"It's not real common around here."

"What about in the service?"

"Maybe. Didn't pay much attention to it if I did."

"Well, you're seein' it now. And evidently you'll be seein' it again Saturday night at the talent show."

"Looks like it."

The song ended. The blue-eyed woman came toward him and stuck out her hand. "Whew! That's a workout. If you haven't guessed, I'm Kendra."

"Pleased to meet you, ma'am." She had a firm handshake. Not surprising since she was Ryker's momma.

"And I'm thrilled you're here, Badger. Let me introduce you to my friends."

He committed the names to memory as she went around the group. The redhead was Deidre, the tall blond was Christine, the short brunette was Judy and the slender woman with short gray hair was Jo, Ryker's honorary aunt.

"We were about to take a break and have something to eat," Kendra said. "Are you hungry?"

"Ma'am, I was born hungry."

She laughed. "That's what I love to hear."

"We're on it, Kendra," Deidre said. "You get Badger settled. We'll handle dishing up the food and opening the wine."

"Will do." Kendra glanced at Ryker. "Or wait. Were you going to take Badger to the hospital Christmas party with you?"

"I was, but he has...other plans. I just need to get his suitcase and duffel out of the truck."

"I'll bring it in." Badger started for the door.

"Wait a sec, Badger." Kendra turned and headed for the hallway. "Cody brought you a coat. Put that on if you're going back out."

"I surely appreciate that he did that."

"He said you could keep it as long as you need to," she said over her shoulder.

"Mighty nice of him."

She returned with a sheepskin jacket similar to Ryker's. "This should fit."

He put it on and sighed. "Perfect. Thank you."

Ryker walked over and gave his mom a kiss on the cheek. "Thanks for everything. I'll walk Badger out and then head on over to the hospital event."

"Sounds good, son. Badger, I'll see you in a minute."

"Yes, ma'am." Buttoning his borrowed coat, Badger followed Ryker out to the truck. "They're a great bunch."

"They are. Known them all my life."

"I envy you that."

Ryker walked with him around to the passenger side. "Yeah, I'll bet you do. How are things at home? We didn't talk about that."

"The same. Dad wants me to enroll in some refresher courses so I can finally take the bar exam and Mom says if I don't do that I'm an ungrateful son who seems determined to throw away my very expensive education and the opportunities I've been given."

Ryker leaned against the side of the truck. "I'm sorry. I was hoping they'd have mellowed while you were gone."

"I was hopin' the same. Evidently they were hopin' I'd have come to my senses. It doesn't leave much middle ground."

"No."

"The plain truth is, I'm an embarrassment to them. All their friends have model kids who've done what was expected." He heaved his suitcase out of the truck. "They didn't run away to join the Air Force like present company."

"Then I'm glad you came here for Christmas. I just wish you hadn't cooked up this scheme with Hayley."

"I know you don't like it." He took his duffel out of the cab. "And you don't believe it'll be fine. But it will." He hoisted the duffel over his shoulder and picked up his suitcase.

"I was planning that we'd take the plane up tomorrow morning, but I suppose this deal of yours could interfere with that."

"I won't let that happen. I want to see the plane. Hell, I want to fly the plane. I was itchin' to take the controls of the one I was on today."

"That's a good sign." Ryker's expression grew more cheerful. "I'll be here at nine."

"I'll be ready."

"Okay. Well, are you all psyched up to go in there and spin your romantic tale?"

"Sure."

"Then I'll leave you to it."

"See you in the mornin'." As he carried his suitcase and duffel up to the porch and Ryker drove away, he rehearsed what he would say to the Whine and Cheese Club. It had to be smooth.

He was on a mission. Hayley was in a fix and she needed him.

* * *

Two hours later, relying on his phone's GPS and directions from the Whine and Cheese ladies, Badger was on the road to town and the parsonage where Hayley's folks lived. Kendra had loaned him her truck, so he was driving with extreme care. Snowdrifts decorated the edges of the road like meringue but the pavement was dry.

Hell of a lot of darkness in the country. Here and there multicolored Christmas lights glowed from a house surrounded by black nothingness. Not much traffic, either. He'd turn on the radio if he knew which button to push.

He'd spent the past two hours joking with Kendra's friends and dancing some hip hop with them. They'd talked about including him in their act, but he was already doing the juggling act so horning in on their segment seemed like overexposure.

Besides, he had enough going on with the Hayley situation. Near as he could tell, they'd bought his story and thought it was very romantic. They'd said Virginia was a little pushy but Warren was a sweetheart. They'd wished him well.

He'd set out as if embarking on a quest. He'd never proposed to a woman, so the concept of potential in-laws, even if they'd never become actual in-laws, was a new challenge. The fact that Hayley's daddy was a preacher made things even more interesting.

But he could handle it. The story he and Hayley had cooked up was convincing. So why was he sweating?

Oh. He'd cranked the heat and now the cab was like an oven. He turned down the heat and cracked a window. Then closed it immediately.

The air coming in was like the freezer compartment of a refrigerator. How did people live in country this cold? How did a rancher like Kendra deal with sub-zero temperatures when she had to leave the house to feed the horses huddled in the barn? Maybe not huddled. The McGavins might heat the barn.

But Kendra had to get from the house to the barn and that couldn't be any fun. His hat would be off to her if he had a hat.

She'd offered him a cap with earflaps but he'd gently turned her down. His borrowed sheepskin jacket looked manly. The cap did not. He wanted to make a good impression on Hayley's parents. On Hayley, too, for that matter.

As he neared town, the houses were closer together and streetlights appeared along the way. Much better. He was used to civilization and lots of it. If he couldn't be near a large metropolis, he wanted to be in a plane headed for one.

That said, Eagles Nest decked out for the holidays was damned cute. Garlands and bows adorned the street lamps on Main Street and all the shops had something festive in the window— wreaths, candy canes, snowflakes and lights. Drifts of snow on windowsills and along building foundations made it look like a tabletop village.

He located the street he was looking for and turned right. His destination was only a couple of blocks down and easy to spot. The church had a steeple and the parsonage had a nativity scene in the front yard.

A silver sedan parked in the driveway had to be Hayley's rental. He had just enough room to pull in behind it without leaving the back of Kendra's truck sticking out in the street.

The house was modest but the Christmas decorations made it look festive. Hayley had said they'd wait dessert for him. As he stepped out of the truck, he was short of breath. It wasn't from the cold, which was milder here than out at the ranch or even at the airport. Might as well face it. He was a tad bit nervous.

He had no reason to be. This wasn't real. All he had to do was walk in there and convince her parents he was in love with their daughter. And that was the problem.

Other than adolescent crushes, which had mostly involved unobtainable movie stars, he'd never considered himself in love. Lust had happened on a regular basis. But finding that special forever connection had been like snipe hunting in the swamp.

How did a guy act when he was in love? Other than what he'd seen in movies, which was mostly fake unless the co-stars had conducted an off-screen romance, he had no clue what his behavior should be. Especially when he was meeting her parents.

He took his time walking around to the porch steps. Maybe he was already making mistakes. A man in love would be eager to meet his girlfriend's folks, wouldn't he? He wouldn't dawdle and then hesitate before pressing the doorbell.

Before he'd accomplished it, the door opened and Hayley stood there smiling at him. Her parents, tall and slender like Hayley, stood behind her. She favored her mom. Even their hair was similar. Her dad had lost most of his hair and wore glasses. They both looked excited to meet their daughter's new guy.

In that moment, he knew exactly what to do. He reached for Hayley and drew her into his arms. "Hello, darlin'. I've missed you somethin' terrible."

4

Hayley hadn't expected Badger to hug her right off the bat. She'd never been in his arms and now it appeared he was about to kiss her in front of her parents.

She wasn't prepared. "I've missed you, too!" Perhaps her voice was a little loud, a little manic, but she was new at this subterfuge thing. "Come in, come in. My folks are dying to meet you." She extricated herself from his grasp and pulled him into the house. "Mom, Dad, meet Badger Calhoun, the answer to my prayers."

His brown eyes sparkled with laughter. "I'm honored that you think of me that way. I'll do my best to live up to it."

"Oh, you already have." She stepped back as her parents approached. "This is my mom, Virginia, and my dad, Warren."

Badger greeted them both with a perfect combination of warmth and deference. After he'd kissed her mom's cheek and exchanged a hearty handshake with her dad, he hung his jacket on the coat tree in the hall and they ushered him into the living room.

"Nice jacket." Hayley took a seat on the couch and patted the spot next to her because that seemed like the right move.

"Borrowed it from Ryker's brother. You were right that I needed one." He sat next to her, laced his fingers through hers and gave a little squeeze.

She squeezed back. He was doing a great job. She was making it up as she went along because she'd never brought a boyfriend home. She'd figured out early on that it would send her mom into stealth wedding mode.

Her mom settled in her easy chair and gazed at them adoringly. "I should be put out with you two for keeping this a secret, but I can't bring myself to be angry. I've waited a long time for Hayley to find Mr. Right, and here you are, Badger. I couldn't be happier."

"I'm mighty glad you're pleased, Mrs. Bennett."

"Oh, do call me Virginia. Unless you'd prefer Mom."

"You know, Virginia's such a pretty name. Always liked it. I'd be honored to call you that, if I may."

Hayley smiled at him. *Nicely played.*

"So, Atlanta, huh?" Her dad sat in his recliner and pushed his glasses against the bridge of his nose. "This must be quite a change for you, coming from a big city in the South to a small town in the dead of winter."

"Definitely, sir."

"Speaking of dead stuff, are you into zombies, son?"

"Dad..." And she'd expected her mom to ask the embarrassing questions.

Badger seemed to take it in stride. "No, sir. Can't say I am. Are you?"

"Yes and no. Years ago, Virginia and I went to Atlanta for a conference. Beautiful city, by the way."

"Thank you. I think so, too."

"Anyway, on our first visit, we took a tour that had a *Gone with the Wind* vibe. But we went to that same conference this fall, and the scheduled tour was about the zombie TV show."

"Yes, sir, I noticed they had those. I've been out of the country the last ten years so I didn't pay a lot of attention. Only watched the show a couple of times because of the Atlanta connection."

"I wasn't into it, either, but we took the tour because it was part of our conference fee."

"It was?" Hayley blinked. "A bunch of ministers scheduled a tour of zombie film locations?"

"Oh, yes, they certainly did." Her mother shuddered. "You would have hated it. Ghastly stuff."

"Virginia wasn't happy, but I was okay with it. Kind of fascinated, in fact. Keeping up with popular culture helps me stay relevant. Anyhow, after going on the plantation tour and then the zombie tour, I can't get this mashup out of my head."

"Warren, I don't think this is the time or place for—"

"What if you combined a zombie apocalypse with *Gone with the Wind?*"

Her mom sighed and shook her head. "Badger, I apologize. He's been going on about his idea ever since we came home."

"Because it's high concept!" Her dad focused on Badger. "Picture it, son. You're from there, so this should resonate with you. Imagine zombie Scarlett raising her fist and delivering her famous line about never going hungry again. Is that not cutting-edge?"

Badger chuckled. "Sure is."

"Can't decide if Rhett Butler should be a zombie or the one fighting the zombies. What do you think?"

"Hard to say. Depends on whether you want to keep the romance between them or ditch it."

"It's iconic. I say keep it."

"Me, too."

"Dad, please tell me you're not working in zombie jokes for the talent show."

He shook his head. "No, sweetheart. That wouldn't fit with my *Holy Hilarity, Godman* theme. But I could keep it in mind in case they do another show next year. What do you think, Badger?"

He smiled at her dad. "Zombies surely would be different."

"I know, right?" Her dad's answering grin was endearingly familiar. "Hey, Badger, what did one zombie say to the other zombie while they ate the comedian?"

"Beats me."

Her dad's grin widened. "He said, *does this taste funny to you?*" Then he cracked up.

So did Badger. It wasn't a polite, fake laugh, either. He was clearly tickled by her dad's goofy humor.

Hayley's mom rolled her eyes before pushing up from her chair. "Time for a change of subject. Who wants dessert?"

That set the guys off again.

Hayley stood. "I'll help." As her dad and Badger began trading zombie jokes, she followed her mom into the kitchen.

Once there, her mom gave her a quick hug. "Oh, honey, he's perfect."

"He is?" She caught herself. "I mean, yes, he certainly is."

"The minute I saw him I knew he was right for you." Her mom took dessert plates out of the cupboard and set them on the counter. "But I never dreamed he'd be the perfect son-in-law for your father. He's going to love having Badger in the family."

"Mom, we're almost engaged, but it's a little early to toss around terms like son-in-law."

"You'll be engaged before this vacation is over. I saw the look in his eye."

"You did?"

"That man's crazy about you." She took a pumpkin pie and a can of whipped cream out of the refrigerator. "Would you please switch on the coffee? It's ready to go." She took a knife out of the wooden block on the counter. "I just wish I could call him Thaddeus. It's so much more elegant."

"But he hates the name." Hayley turned on the coffee pot and took mugs down from the cabinet above it.

"How can he? He's named after his father and grandfather!"

Hayley had considered that, too, especially after finding out that he'd chosen Eagles Nest over Atlanta for his first stateside Christmas. But she wasn't willing to share her speculations with her mother. "Maybe he was teased in school."

"I suppose he could have been. Kids will do that." Her mom sliced the pie. "But I love that kind of tradition. I wanted to name Luke after your father but he wouldn't hear of it. He's never been overly fond of his name, either. I guess I should be grateful he doesn't want to be called Raccoon or Porcupine."

"I like Badger. It's—"

"Did I hear my name mentioned?" The man in question appeared in the kitchen doorway.

She looked over at him. Sure enough, he was standing smack dab under the mistletoe. Her mother always hung it there to go with her holiday apron that said *Kiss the Cook*. "I was just saying to Mom that I like your nickname."

"And I don't *dislike* it," her mother said. "But I think your given name has a certain ring to it. I hope you're planning to use it on the wedding invitations."

Hayley gulped. "Mom, we haven't exactly—"

"Don't worry." He gave her a quick glance. "We'll use it on the invitations."

"Oh, good."

"The pie looks amazin'. I came in to see if I could carry anything in for you."

"That would be lovely." Her mom glanced at him. "Hayley," she said in a sing-song voice. "Look where he's standing."

"What?" He turned right and then left. "Is this a bad place?"

"Oh, no, you're in the exact right place," her mom said. "Go on, Hayley. Claim your kiss."

He looked up and spied the mistletoe. "Aha." Amusement flickered in his eyes as Hayley approached. "Guess I'm caught."

"Seems like it." She couldn't be tentative about this kiss if she wanted her mom to believe they were madly in love. Her heart beat so loud she was scared he could hear it or worse yet, her mom could.

Arms at his sides, he watched her.

"First time under the mistletoe." She slid her palms up his solid chest. The guy had some serious muscles. And surprise, surprise, his heart was going fast, too.

"Then you best make it good, darlin'."

She stepped closer and gazed into eyes that had darkened to the color of rich chocolate. "Can't make it too good with Mom in the room."

"You two lovebirds just pretend I'm not here."

His mouth twitched as if he might be holding back laughter. Great mouth. Full. Sensuous. Dizzy with anticipation, she raised up on tiptoe and pressed her lips against his.

Oh, boy. In trouble, now. Velvet. Yielding. Supple. Pleasure source. Want more... Danger, danger!

Stepping back with a gasp, she unclenched her fingers from his shirt. Whoops. Got a little carried away.

Slowly he opened his eyes. Heat flared as he held her gaze.

She swallowed. "Merry Christmas."

"Same to you." His voice was husky.

"Whew!" Her mom giggled. "That was the hottest mistletoe kiss I've ever seen!"

"What's going on in here?" Her dad appeared behind Badger.

"Just our happy couple enjoying their first Christmas, Warren. Remember our first Christmas?"

"Like it was yesterday. You had that red knit dress. Take it from me, Badger, a blond in red on Christmas Eve is hard to resist."

"I believe you." He glanced at Hayley. "Did you pack a red dress?"

"I did not." A red flannel nightgown, but he'd never see that.

"So," her dad said. "Are we having pumpkin pie or not?"

"We're having it." Her mom picked up the can of whipped cream and quickly placed a frothy layer of white on each piece. "Grab your pie, pour yourself some coffee, and off we go. There's cream in the fridge if you need it, Badger."

"Thank you, ma'am. I take it black."

Hayley made a note. It was something she should already know if she expected to pull off this charade.

That kiss hadn't been a charade, though. She wouldn't have to fake her attraction to this guy. "I'll take some, though. Thanks, Mom." She was the only one in the family who liked cream in her coffee. Her mother always remembered to stock it when she came to visit.

Little things like that touched her heart. She could appreciate them more when she wasn't fending off would-be suitors her mother had lined up. So far Badger's plan was working out exactly as planned.

Mostly. She'd expected to enjoy getting to know him better. She hadn't expected that one kiss with virtually no body contact other than a lip-lock would inspire fantasies of naked time alone with him.

Dream on, girlfriend. He was staying at the ranch and she was staying with her parents. Still, it was fun to think about.

Once they were back in the living room with pie and coffee, her mom began organizing the troops. She glanced at Badger. "Hayley said besides coming to meet us, you're also here to see Ryker McGavin."

"Yes, ma'am. He and I served together. By the way, this pie is delicious. Pumpkin is my favorite."

"Hayley's, too, but I'm sure you knew that."

"I'm not sure he did, Mom." Might as well lay the groundwork for future slipups. "When you carry on a long-distance relationship, you don't find out quite as much about each other."

"I understand and I'm sure you'll figure out a solution so you can be together all the time. Love finds a way."

Badger glanced over at Hayley. "We're workin' on it, right, darlin'?"

"Sure are." She needed some term of endearment for him. Or not. If she hadn't used one so far it might seem weird if she started calling him by a cutsie name now.

Her mom put down her coffee mug. "I don't want to make things difficult for either of you during this holiday. I remember early in our marriage Warren and I had to figure out how to appease both families as they competed for our time. So, Badger, tell me what you already have going with Ryker and the McGavins and we'll work from there."

"Kendra's plannin' a big family dinner tomorrow night. She's asked if Hayley can come, but I didn't make any promises. I need to be there, though."

"Of course you do. And Hayley should, too. You're a couple, after all."

Hayley was used to her mother making decisions for her but tonight she decided to assert herself. "I don't have to go over there, Mom. If you have some activity in mind, let me know."

"I had a plan but I've scrapped that now that everything's changed. I think it would be great if you went to Kendra's tomorrow night and got acquainted, since Ryker and Badger are such close friends."

"All right, then."

"In the morning we could go shopping in town. I still need a couple of things. Then we can have lunch at the Guzzling Grizzly. You're welcome to come along, Badger."

"Thank you, ma'am, but Ryker and I are takin' the Beechcraft up in the mornin'."

Her dad put down his coffee. "I'll be doggone. So that's where Ryker got the name. I've seen the ads for his commuter service but I couldn't figure out why he called it Badger Air. I like it, though. It's funny. That logo with the badger wearing a World War I leather helmet is hysterical."

Badger chuckled. "Yeah, it is. I was still deployed when he had that designed. He sent me a picture and I tacked it up in the barracks. The guys loved it."

"I'll bet." Her dad picked up his coffee again. "I may be making a leap, but are you two in business together?"

"In a way. I'm more of a silent partner."

"Nice." Her dad sipped his coffee. "You planning to do any flying now that you're out of the service?"

"That's still up in the air."

Her dad laughed. "Good one." He sent a smile in her direction. "I like this guy. He has my cornball sense of humor. You have my permission to keep him around."

"Thanks, Dad." His happy expression made her heart ache. She'd expected her mom to be over the moon regarding the new development but she hadn't figured on her dad taking such a shine to Badger. Damn.

5

How ironic. Within the first ten minutes of meeting Hayley's dad, Badger had established an easy camaraderie that he'd never achieved with his own father. Then again, the two men couldn't be more different. Hayley's dad was open and curious about life, whereas his father was closed off to anything that didn't fit his rigid worldview. He rarely smiled or laughed and yet that seemed to be Warren Bennett's default setting.

As for Warren's daughter, Badger was having very inappropriate thoughts about her thanks to that mistletoe encounter. She'd given him a definite buzz and she hadn't even used her tongue. He wanted more of that, and yet this romance was only pretend, right?

"Can you be here Friday night, Badger?"

He brought his attention back to the conversation and Virginia's question. "That should be fine. Nothing was mentioned about Friday night. I think it's clear."

"That's good, because Luke's coming in Friday afternoon. You'll want to meet him."

"I'm looking forward to it." Who was Luke, again?

"Can't wait to see that brother of mine," Hayley said.

Thank you, Hayley. "I'm eager to meet him."

Virginia looked at her daughter. "Did you tell Luke about Badger? I know sometimes you and your brother tell each other things you don't tell your dad and me."

"I didn't say anything to him, Mom."

"Then isn't he going to be surprised?"

Her dad finished off his coffee. "You'll like him, Badger. Luke's a good guy."

"He must be if he's part of this family."

Virginia beamed at him. "What a lovely thing to say. So, we're set for Friday, and I assume we'll all be going to the talent show at the Guzzling Grizzly on Saturday night. There's a candlelight service at the church Sunday night."

"Sounds nice." He'd always been fond of going to church on Christmas Eve.

"I behave myself for that one," her dad said. "It's special."

"I'm sure it is." He was looking forward to all the events, which beat any Christmas he'd had in a long time, maybe ever. The only downside was that he and Hayley would be in a crowd the whole time. He'd like to find out if that kiss was a fluke but he didn't see any opportunities lurking in the schedule.

"I don't know how you'll manage Christmas Day, though," Virginia said. "We'd love to have you here, of course, but I'm sure you'll also want to spend time with Ryker and the rest of the McGavins."

He took Hayley's hand again and glanced over at her. "We'll figure it out, won't we, darlin'?"

"Absolutely. Listen, you've had a long day. What time is it in Atlanta, now?"

"Two hours later than here." Hayley might be wanting to shuffle him out the door and catch her breath. He was okay with that, although tonight had been more fun than he'd expected.

"Oh, my." Virginia stood. "I forgot about the time difference and travel can really tire you out. We shouldn't keep you any longer."

"I've enjoyed every minute." He got up and so did Hayley. "It's been a pleasure meetin' y'all."

"The pleasure's ours." Virginia walked over and hugged him.

"My wife is right, as always." Warren left his chair and laid a hand on his shoulder. "Like she said earlier, Hayley's taken her time finding someone. I'm glad she waited until you came along, son."

"Thanks." Badger's throat tightened, which was stupid. He cleared it. "I'm mighty glad she did, too."

Hayley touched his arm. "I'll walk you out."

"That would be great."

After he'd said more goodbyes and he and Hayley had put on their coats, he followed her through the front door with his jacket unbuttoned.

Big mistake. An icy breeze sliced through his cotton shirt in two seconds. He quickly let go of her hand so he could remedy the situation.

Her laughter created a tiny cloud in the freezing air. "It's cold in Montana." She'd zipped up her fur-lined parka to her neck and put up the hood. The breeze turned her cheeks and her nose pink. Cute as hell.

"Guess I should start listenin' to you."

"You definitely should." Hands shoved in her pockets, she started down the steps. "How did it go at the ranch? I've been wondering how everything turned out with Ryker's family."

"Fine." Bits of ice crunched under his feet as he followed her over to the driveway. "Shouldn't be any issues there."

"Good to hear. I see you managed to get some wheels."

"Kendra's truck. She was nice enough to loan it to me. She said I could have it whenever I needed it. There are several vehicles at the ranch so it's not a problem."

"That's handy." She paused beside the truck and gazed at him. "Good job in there, by the way. My folks really like you."

"I like them, too. But I can see what you mean about your momma. Her comment about the invitations clued me in. She's really focused on the weddin' end of it."

"I predict she'll have more to say on the subject as the days go by. She's convinced you're head over heels in love with me."

"That's what we want, right?"

"Yep, and you're very convincing. Did you take drama classes in school?"

"No, no classes." The discussion irritated him a little. "Just so you know, it's not totally fake.

I don't want you to think I'm forcin' myself to do this. You're very attractive. Don't forget that I was goin' to ask you out before we settled on this idea."

"That's true, you were. And I'm grateful that you suggested it. Those plans Mom scrapped were setups. Otherwise she wouldn't have had to cancel them."

"I picked up on that." The jacket kept him reasonably warm but the top of his head prickled with cold.

"So Kendra bought the story?"

"Sure did. Her Whine and Cheese Club was there, so they all got to hear it, too. By now news of our romance has probably spread to—"

"What club is that?"

"Whine and Cheese. Like wine only with an H."

"I get it. Cute. This little town has a lot of charm to it."

"I can already see that. If I were into small towns, this would be great, but I'm used to a big city."

"Me, too. Besides, like I said on the plane, my mom and I would come to blows over this wedding thing if I relocated to Eagles Nest."

"But we can soak up the ambiance while we're here." His forehead was going numb but he was having a good time watching her blue eyes sparkle in the Christmas lights. He hated to leave. He'd warm up once he got back in the truck.

"I think I'll enjoy soaking it up this year more than I ever did before. I owe you."

"Nah. It's fun for me."

"I hope so." She stepped closer. "Don't look now, but I think the living room curtain just moved."

"Your momma's spyin' on us?"

"I guarantee it's not my dad pulling back that curtain. He's strictly live and let live."

"So I gathered. He's a great guy. You're lucky."

"I know. But if she's watching out the window, you should probably kiss me."

Oh, yeah, life was good. He smiled. "Gee, do I have to?"

"Shut up. You liked the mistletoe kiss. I could tell."

"I loved the mistletoe kiss. I was hopin' you might want to try that again sometime."

"I wouldn't mind." She gazed up at him. "And it would be what Mom's expecting to see."

"Then let's give our audience what they want. But first I need to set the stage." He unzipped her parka.

"What are you doing?"

"We need more body contact. We'll stay warmer that way." He unbuttoned his coat.

"We won't, either. We'll freeze our—"

"Come here." Sliding his hands inside her coat, he pulled her close and lowered his head.

"You're insane."

"You need to put your arms inside my coat, too."

"You've obviously never made out in cold country or you'd know this isn't a good idea."

"I haven't made out in the cold, but I saw a movie where two people got naked to keep from freezing to death."

"We're not getting naked." She slipped her arms inside his coat and snuggled against him.

"More's the pity." He closed the gap and claimed her sweet mouth. The flavors were two of his favorites, whipped cream and pumpkin pie.

But that didn't explain the jolt of pleasure that traveled along his nerve endings as he began to explore with his tongue. She might have sassed him about the way he'd approached this kiss, but her mouth was hot and eager.

Thanks to eliminating some layers, he enjoyed the sensation of her breasts cushioning the space between them. And he discovered that her heart was thumping as fast as his. When her tongue thrust into his mouth, he grew bold enough to cup her ass and pull her in tight so she'd know exactly how she was affecting him.

She moaned and wiggled closer. Good sign. He delved deeper with his tongue and their rapid breathing fogged the air. Maybe it was still cold outside. He couldn't say.

He lost track of his surroundings as he immersed himself in her kiss and the heat pouring from her body. He needed her, and she was giving every indication of needing him, too.

Reaching under her sweater, he searched for the back clasp of her bra.

Gasping, she broke away from his kiss and backed up a couple of feet. "Badger!"

He sucked in air. "What?"

"You can't unhook my bra in the driveway of the parsonage. It's just not done."

"Then let's move to the neighbor's driveway."

She stared at him and then she began to smile. "You really are insane."

He took a shaky breath and smiled back. "You told me to kiss you."

"So I did."

"Do you think that kiss will satisfy your momma?"

"I should hope so."

"Did it satisfy you?"

Her gaze was hot as she zipped her parka. "Not by a long shot."

"Then maybe we can continue this another time."

"I don't see how that would work." She shoved her hands back in her pockets. "At least not the way we've set up our visit."

"You know what? If we were actually lovers, we would have figured this out. We wouldn't have come here for Christmas without a plan for bein' alone at least sometimes."

"That's a very good point. Will it make anyone suspicious if we haven't factored that in?"

"Do you want to factor it in?"

She blushed. "I'd like to consider it as an option."

"So would I, darlin'. So would I."

"Maybe we're dealing with the power of suggestion. We're supposed to be hot for each other, so now we are."

"I don't think so, but we could test it. I'll just have to kiss you again tomorrow."

"Might not have a chance."

"I'll make a chance." He gave her a quick peck on the cheek. "See you then." Climbing in the truck, he closed the door and drove away. He was at least a mile down the road before he remembered to turn on the heater.

6

Although Hayley would have loved to walk around the block to settle down after that lollapalooza of a kiss, her parents would worry if she didn't come back in right away. She took several deep breaths, slipped inside and hung her parka on the coat tree.

Her mom, the spymaster, sat in her easy chair wearing her reading glasses and pretending total absorption in a book. Hayley would almost buy it if the book weren't upside down. Her dad, who'd received intel from the spymaster, leafed through a journal from one of the many organizations he'd joined. His reading material was right-side up.

She returned to her seat on the couch and folded her hands in her lap. "I hope Badger and I didn't break any house rules or shock your neighbors just now."

Her mom glanced up, innocence personified. "Were you doing something shocking out there?"

"Maybe. Depends on how strict you two are these days. I remember getting lectured about that very thing once upon a time."

Her dad put aside his journal and nudged his glasses into place. "Yes, well you were seventeen and I was a lot more worried about appearances back then. I've loosened up."

She grinned at him. "Good to know, Dad."

"I think it's lovely that you two are so passionate." Her mom laid her book on her lap. "And tasteful about it, too. Some young couples can't keep their hands off each other even though other people are around."

"Well, we are both over thirty. Let's hope we've developed some restraint."

"That kiss didn't look very restrained." Then her mother blushed. "Sorry. I only took a quick peek."

"It's okay, Mom."

"It's just that I'm so happy for you. I meant to ask this before, but have you met his parents?"

"Not yet."

"Has he told them about you?"

"No, but—"

"Really? Not a word?"

"Isn't it better to deliver that kind of info in person? Don't you think that's better, Dad?"

"Mostly, but if you wait too long they might not be too happy."

"Oh, we won't." *Spin it girl, spin it.* "But it was logical to start with you guys because of the Eagles Nest connection."

Her mother nodded. "To think that you had this town in common. What are the chances?"

"Kismet."

"I know. So romantic. Still I wish I knew more about his side of the family. I mean, if we're going to be related, it would nice to—"

"I'm sure he'll be happy to tell you." Or not. "I don't know all that much, myself. It's like we've been enclosed in this bubble of bliss, oblivious to the rest of the world."

Her mother sighed. "Just like your dad and I were. Remember, Warren?"

"It's called being snowbound, Virginia. We couldn't get out and nobody could get in."

"Yes! It was a bubble of snow! Every young couple should be lucky like that. By the time they dug us out, we were engaged."

"If we hadn't been your dad would have come after me with a shotgun."

She laughed. "Go ahead and joke about it but you wanted to get married as much as I did."

He smiled at her. "Yeah. Best decision I ever made. But, since Hayley and Badger aren't snowbound, and we're in the digital age, let's find out some basics about his parents." He picked up his phone from the lamp table next to his recliner.

"Dad! That feels like snooping."

"I agree and I promise not to let Badger know I looked this up. But since your mother brought up the subject, I'm curious." He spoke into the phone. "Find information on Thaddeus Livingston Calhoun the second in Atlanta, Georgia."

"This seems wrong. Mom, doesn't this seem wrong?"

"No, dear, it's a great idea."

"But—"

A melodious woman's voice stopped her cold. *Information located.*

"Let's see what it says." Her dad began to read. "Thaddeus Livingston Calhoun the Second, fifty-eight, is a senior partner in the law firm of Calhoun, Lipcott and Gervais. He's married to the former Stella Louise Jorgenson, fifty-six. They have one son, Thaddeus Livingston Calhoun the third, thirty-three."

Her dad clicked off the phone and set it back on the lamp table. "That's enough. At least we know they're gainfully employed. Or rather, Thaddeus is."

All of it was news to Hayley. During the flight, she'd been so focused on preparing Badger for her family that she hadn't asked about his, not even whether he had siblings. Evidently he was an only child born to what sounded like highly educated and likely affluent parents.

Her dad glanced at her mom. "Does that help, Virginia?"

"It does, but now I have so many questions. Hayley, you said he'd been in the service for ten years so that means he didn't enlist until he was twenty-three. Do you know what he was doing between high school and enlisting?"

"I, um, no, I don't. Not really. Like I said, we haven't spent nearly as much time together as couples who live in the same city."

"I wonder why he didn't become a lawyer like his father?"

"I'm sure it's because he loves to fly. But you won't ask him that, right? Because we don't want him to know Dad looked up his parents on the Internet."

"I suppose not. It is better if we let him tell us of his own accord."

"Absolutely." And her mom would make a dash for the computer the minute she had a private moment. "That includes anything else you might find out online." She must have a lot of her mother in her, after all, because now she was tempted to look him up, too.

"Okay."

"I won't announce that I looked up his folks online," her dad said. "But I'd be surprised if he didn't expect me to research both him and his parents. That's what people do these days."

"I know, Dad."

"You should do the same."

"Maybe. But I'd rather hear these things from him." Besides, she'd only be satisfying her idle curiosity by researching him. After the holidays, she had no plans to see him again.

"You're in love." Her dad's gaze was filled with kindness and understanding. "You want to respect his privacy. I get that. I'm not in love with him and my darling daughter is considering marriage after only spending a few weekends with the guy."

"Quality weekends."

"I'm sure they have been. I trust your judgment and your instincts, but obtaining a little basic info like finding out who his parents are eases my mind somewhat."

"I'm sure it does."

"Don't get me wrong. He made a great first impression and I can see how you two would get along. Christmas is a traditional time for couples to get engaged and you may decide to do that. But I would advise making it a long engagement so you can be sure you know each other before you take that big step."

"Very good advice, Dad." And that was why he was good at what he did. She had a new respect for his ability to be warm and welcoming while also intelligently assessing a situation and watching for potential issues. It was what she tried to do in her work with senior citizens. She'd learned a lot from her dad, more than she might have realized.

Her mom sighed. "It is good advice. But I'm dying to plan their wedding, Warren."

He laughed. "Tell me something I don't know."

* * *

Badger had always been vulnerable to jet lag. It prompted him to wake up at six in the morning. Still very dark outside.

He couldn't fault the accommodations, though. Cody's old bedroom was cozy and the mattress was extra-long so his feet didn't hang off the end the way they usually did in most beds other than the one in his room at his folks' house.

He tried to go back to sleep, but eventually he couldn't lie there another second. Dressing quickly, he skipped shaving and went down the dark hallway, through the living room and into the kitchen.

Kendra had anticipated that he'd be awake early. She'd set up the coffee pot so all he had to do was turn it on. A loaf of bread sat on the counter along with an unopened jar of peanut butter and a table knife so he could make himself some breakfast.

He switched on the coffee, put bread in the toaster, and grabbed a banana from the bowl of fruit in the middle of the small kitchen table. He sat there to eat it until the toast and coffee were ready.

The gurgling coffee pot was the only sound in the room. He'd never been surrounded by so much stillness and it was a little spooky. His parents' house was in Buckhead, an exclusive area, but traffic noise still penetrated the hedges enclosing the opulent estate where he'd grown up.

Once he'd finished and cleaned up his mess, he put on his borrowed jacket, unlocked the front door, and stepped outside. He counted it an act of bravery because he knew it would be ass-freezing cold out there.

He did it anyway. He'd always heard that ranches woke up at dawn, and he wanted to see that for himself. Since it wasn't dawn, yet, he should be able to watch the entire show.

Shivering despite the borrowed coat, he sat on the porch steps and waited. Eventually a sliver of light appeared on the horizon, but the wreaths still glittered over the double doors on both barns. He'd brought his phone so he pulled it out of his jacket pocket and tried to capture the magic of those wreaths.

He'd guess the wreaths were hooked into an outlet designed for security lights. For the holidays, though, the space was reserved for a bit of fantasy, instead. Mounting those wreaths would have taken some effort and a very tall ladder. He admired the enthusiasm for the season.

A truck chugged down the dirt road toward the ranch. Badger's phone said it was seven-thirty, still full dark, and here was someone arriving, presumably to work. These ranch people were dedicated.

The driver parked in the area near the house. Badger walked over to introduce himself and satisfy his curiosity about who would voluntarily show up at this hour ready to work. The military kept this kind of schedule but soldiers didn't have a choice.

A tall, lanky man climbed down from the truck. He wore boots, jeans, a blue plaid flannel shirt and a sheepskin coat like the one Badger had borrowed. His hat looked worn, but at least he had one. As the cold prickled Badger's scalp, he envied that cowboy his hat.

The guy spotted him and called out. "Hey, there. I'll bet you're Ryker's Air Force friend."

"How could you tell?" He was getting used to the puffs of fog that appeared during an outdoor conversation.

"Couldn't be anyone else. You're the only guest staying at the ranch this Christmas. I see you borrowed Cody's jacket. He should've given you a hat, too."

"I don't think Ryker asked him for a hat."

"We can remedy that situation." He stuck out his hand. "Welcome to Wild Creek Ranch. I'm Jim Underwood, Faith's dad."

"Badger Calhoun." The guy had a calloused working man's hand and a firm grip.

"Come on down to the barn, Badger. There's always been a spare hat in the tack room. Bet it's still there."

"I'd be mighty grateful to borrow it until I can buy my own." He fell into step beside Jim.

"Faith and Cody should be along any time now to start feeding. You met them, yet?"

"No, sir. Just Kendra and the Whine and Cheese ladies."

Jim chuckled. "What did you think of that bunch?"

"They're a hoot."

"Aren't they, though. A Christmas rap song for the talent show." Jim shook his head. "You never know what they'll get up to next."

"I saw it. They're doin' a decent job."

"They could do a prize-winning job and I wouldn't know the difference. But I'll get a charge out of watching them, anyway."

"Are you here to help Cody and Faith feed the horses?"

"No, I need to do some repair work on the harness for the sleigh."

Badger perked up. "A sleigh like the one in the *Jingle Bells* song?"

"Like that, only this is a two-horse sleigh. I came across it when I attended an auction. After a bunch of texts between Kendra and me, I convinced her the ranch needed an extra revenue stream during the winter months."

"You give people sleigh rides?"

"That's the idea."

"I've always wanted to find out what that's like." He wouldn't mind inviting Hayley for a sleigh ride.

"Then we'll have to set one up for you."

"Is the sleigh in the barn?"

"Yeah, but not this barn. There was more room for it in the new one. The hat I was thinking of is in here, though." He slid aside a wooden bar holding the double doors closed, walked into the barn and flipped on the lights. "Good morning, ladies and gentlemen."

All along the aisle, horses poked their heads out to gaze at Jim and Badger. One, a handsome butterscotch Paint on the far end, whinnied and tossed his head.

"Yeah, yeah, Winston," Jim called out. "I know you're starving to death down there."

The horse responded with a loud snort.

"Don't worry, buddy. There's a hay flake in your future." Jim glanced at Badger. "Winston likes to carry on a conversation."

"He's an eye-catchin' horse."

"That he is. Do you ride?"

"English. But I wouldn't mind tryin' a Western saddle while I'm out here."

"It'll feel like an easy chair after that little bit of leather you're used to. If you go out with Ryker, ask him to put you on Winston. He has a smooth gait."

"I'll surely remember that." He followed Jim into the tack room and breathed in the familiar scent of oiled leather. But the saddles were a complete change from what he was used to. Walking over to a particularly elaborate one, he traced the intricate tooling in the caramel-colored leather. "What a beauty."

"Isn't it?" Pride rang in Jim's voice. "Cody got that for Faith last month. She objected to him spending his hard-earned money on an engagement ring, so he bought her the prettiest saddle he could find."

Badger smiled. "I can't wait to meet a woman who prefers a saddle to a diamond ring."

"She'll be along any minute, now." He picked up a hat sitting brim-side-up on a shelf. After slapping it against his thigh a couple of times to knock the dust off, he handed it to Badger. "See if this fits. I don't know who it belonged to. One of the boys probably donated it to the cause so we'd have a spare out here."

"Thanks." He took the hat by the crown and settled it on his head. "Perfect." His scalp immediately was warmer.

"It's a little beat up, but I personally like 'em better that way. New hats might look snappy, but one with some miles on it sits easier on a man's head, in my opinion."

"Makes sense." He tugged the brim a little lower. "Feels like I've been wearin' it forever." Funny how this hat affected him. As if he'd finally found the right headgear.

Jim nudged back his own hat and studied him. "Looks that way on you, too. You oughta keep it."

"But then you won't have a spare in the tack room."

"We can round up another one. I have a couple at home I hardly ever wear. I can bring over—ah, I hear Faith and Cody coming in. Let's go say howdy."

Badger followed him out of the tack room and came face-to-face with his first cowgirl. Faith wore basically the same thing Cody had on – boots, jeans, flannel shirt, sheepskin jacket and a well-worn Stetson.

"Cody and Faith," Jim said, "meet Badger Calhoun."

Badger snatched off his hat as Faith thrust out her hand. "Pleased to meet you, Badger. I love your name."

"Thank you, ma'am. I was just admirin' your new saddle."

"Isn't it gorgeous?" Her smile revealed a cute little gap between her front teeth. The absence of makeup and a sprinkling of freckles made her look like a teenager. But her handshake was as strong as Jim's. "Cody outdid himself."

"That was exactly my plan." Cody stepped forward and offered his hand. "Good to meet you, Badger. Did Ryker tell you about the juggling?"

"He did. Sounds like fun." Badger met Cody's friendly gaze. His eyes were the same blue as Ryker's and his hair was the same color, too, but there the resemblance ended.

People who glanced at Ryker might have the urge to take a step back. The guy was naturally intimidating, whereas Cody likely caused people to take a step forward, especially women. He looked like he could be in the movies.

"We should set up a practice or two," Cody said. "But I hear through the grapevine that your time will be limited."

Ryker had warned him that gossip would spread, and it had. "We'll find time. I'll need to. I haven't juggled since—" Winston's loud whinny cut him off. "That's one hungry horse." He put his hat back on. "Need help feedin' these critters?"

"Sure. We can always use an extra hand." Cody glanced at him. "Ryker's old hat suits you."

"It was Ryker's?"

"Yep. He left it behind when he went in the service, said we could keep it in the barn as a spare."

"Oh." If the hat had history, no way was he keeping it. "I'm just borrowing it until I can buy my own today."

"You're not gonna find one that has that much character. Ryker doesn't want it anymore or he would have laid claim when he came back. You should keep it."

"That's what I told him," Jim said. "Sometimes the man finds the hat and sometimes the hat finds the man. This one has your name written all over it."

<u>7</u>

Hayley's mom insisted on driving when they set out on their shopping trip. It didn't seem as if it would be a problem until she continued through town instead of finding a place to park.

"Mom, you missed a couple of good spots in front of—"

"I have a better idea than shopping in Eagles Nest. We have plenty of time. Let's go to Bozeman, instead."

"Why?"

"More places to shop. I'd like to get you something special to wear for your dinner with the McGavins."

"That's a nice thought, but it's not necessary. I brought plenty of clothes. Besides, I thought you wanted to shop for Luke. I need to get him something more, too. I only have one present for him and he always comes loaded. I want to look in that collectibles shop. Last year they had some rare books and I want to see if they have any of the Black Stallion series. We used to love those."

"Bozeman has a used bookstore. At least I think they do. If you can find a phone number, you could call and ask if they have any copies."

Hayley left her phone in her purse. Something wasn't right about this change of plans. "You're not suggesting this because Bozeman has a bridal shop, are you?"

Her mother laughed. "You know me too well."

Boy, did she ever. "Mom, I love you to pieces, but despite my unending devotion, I'm not going to try on dresses today."

"Oh, you don't have to. We'll just look. Wouldn't that be fun?"

"Hey, this is me, your tomboy daughter Hayley. The one who would rather take a sharp stick in the eye than try on clothes. I don't even like trying on jeans, let alone some ginormous frock that looks like it belonged to Scarlett O'Hara." Thanks to her dad and Badger, she had Scarlett on the brain.

"You really don't want to do it?"

"No, I really don't want to do it."

Her mother took a deep breath. "Okay. It was worth a shot." She turned off at the next exit and started back toward Eagles Nest. "But I worry that you'll end up getting married in your jeans, now that you mention it."

"That's not a bad idea."

"It's a *terrible* idea. This is your day to shine, to be a princess."

"Once again, allow me to introduce you to your daughter Hayley Renee, the one who played with trucks in the dirt with her little brother instead of dressing up in her mother's outfits and high heels."

"I know, but you're going to be *married.* Think about that magical moment after the bridesmaids and your maid of honor walk down the aisle. The music swells. Everyone stands. Badger's face is alight with anticipation and love. And you appear on the arm of your father in a beautiful..." She swallowed. "A beautiful white dress."

"Mom, are you getting choked up?"

She cleared her throat. "Just a little. I see it so clearly. Always have. I just didn't have a face to put on the groom. Now I do. Oh, honey, can you picture Badger in a tux? Will he not be drop-dead gorgeous?"

Hayley sighed. "Yeah." The image was delicious.

"He'll look amazing."

"Yeah, he will." Oh, wait. She wasn't ever going to see Badger in a tux, especially not standing at the end of the church aisle waiting for her to walk toward him.

"Are you sure you don't want to go look at dresses? I can turn around again."

"I'm sure, Mom. As Scarlett famously said, *tomorrow is another day.*"

"Tomorrow won't work for a shopping trip. It's the twenty-second. We're baking Christmas cookies like we always do."

"I didn't literally mean tomorrow. Let's just wait until after I'm officially engaged to Badger, okay?"

"Okay. Next week will be better, anyway. They might have some good sales between Christmas and New Year's. So, do you want me to tell you what I found out online last night about your sweetheart?"

"No."

"Are you sure?" She looked over at Hayley with a cat-who-ate-the-cream smile.

"All right. But it stays in this car."

"Goes without saying. Anyway, guess how he spent his years between high school and enlisting in the Air Force?"

"Dancing at Chippendales?"

Her mother snorted. "Now I have that image in my head, thank you very much."

"You're welcome." The joke was on her because now she did, too.

"He was enrolled in pre-law at Georgetown University."

"I guess that's not so shocking when you consider his dad's a senior partner in a law firm."

"And his father must do very well for himself. That school costs a fortune."

"Did he graduate?"

"He did. Took him five years, which isn't so unusual these days, but I couldn't find any mention of academic achievements. Considering his family background, I would have expected him to excel."

"Maybe his heart wasn't in it. I don't think you get to fly jets for the Air Force unless you're exceptional."

"Exactly. Chances are he partied his way through his very expensive education, one he probably didn't give a hoot about."

"Did you tell Dad about this?"

"Didn't have to. We looked it up together."

She should have known they would. "Clearly he doesn't want to be a lawyer."

"Clearly." Her mom tapped her finger against the steering wheel. "But I'll bet his father wanted him to. Maybe his mother, too."

"And then he added insult to injury by spending ten years in the Air Force."

"Yep."

Hayley sighed. "That would be sad, if they're at odds over his future. Poor guy."

"It would explain why he hasn't told you anything about them, or taken you to meet them, for that matter. He could be worried about how they'd treat you if they're still upset with him."

"Maybe."

"But isn't he lucky to have found you!"

"He is? How do you figure?"

"It's obvious. I'm sure you don't care whether he becomes a lawyer or not."

"No, I just want him to be happy." Where had *that* come from?

"Of course you do, and so do we. Our family will love him no matter what he chooses to do. We're going to be a very good influence on that boy, Hayley. A very good influence."

"You'll be careful with this information, right? No telling how he views his college years. I don't want him to find out that you and dad dug into his past."

"He won't find out. We'll wait for him to confide in us."

"Good."

* * *

"She handles like a dream." Badger banked to the left and grinned at Ryker sitting in the co-pilot's seat. "You did good when you found her, Cowboy."

"Glad you like her. Thought you would. By the way, I've been trolling the Internet the past month or so. I've found a couple of others with a similar price tag. They might be worth checking out. 'Course that means we'd need another pilot. Know where I could find one?"

"Stitch is comin' out in another three months. Once he gets stateside, he might be interested."

"I wasn't thinking about Stitch."

"I know you weren't." He took a deep breath. "It's an appealin' prospect in some respects, but I don't know if I could handle this winter weather."

"Are you really that much of a pansy-ass that you can't handle a few snowflakes?"

"I just might be. There's another thing. I'm used to a big city with all the amenities. Eagles Nest is chock-a-block with small-town charm, but you don't have a single restaurant that lists sushi on the menu. I checked."

"So you have to drive to Bozeman to get your sushi. Is that a deal breaker? If it is, I'll learn to make your precious raw fish treats with my own two hands and deliver them personally to your lodgings."

"It would almost be worth movin' here to watch you do that."

"I swear I would. At least once, anyway. What else does your spoiled-rotten self require?"

"What if I want grits 'n' gravy at two in the mornin'?"

"I could do that, too. It would make me nauseous but I could do it."

"How about a foam-topped draft at three a.m.?"

"I'll bribe my brother to open the GG just for you."

"But look at all the trouble you'd go to. Atlanta is open twenty-four-seven. When I was comin' home from Hayley's last night around ten, I spotted a crew rollin' up the sidewalk."

"I concede your point, city boy. Eagles Nest is not a bustling metropolis, thank God. I'd hate to see it become one."

"See, that's where we're like night and day. Let me keep on bein' your silent partner and come visit you a couple of times a year to check on the state of our business."

"There are two problems with that. Number one, I'm particular when it comes to who flies for the company. Stitch might work out, but I don't know a better pilot than you."

That knocked him back. "Hard to believe."

"But true. I flew with a lot of guys in ten years. Nobody has your instincts. Well, except me."

Badger laughed. "Still modest as ever."

"Am I right? Do you know a better pilot than me?"

"Yeah, and you're lookin' at him."

"Okay, I'll give you that if you'll come fly with me. We'll make a hell of a team."

His chest tightened. That kind of praise from a man he admired more than anyone he knew was powerful stuff. "What's the second thing?"

"After getting out, you went back to Atlanta. I can't help being curious. You planning on staying? Finding work there?"

That was a sore point. Atlanta was familiar. He knew his way around. Sure, it had changed, but it was still home. Sort of. "Haven't decided. Still thinkin' on it."

"Dangerous path to walk, my friend, especially for a guy who doesn't really need a job."

"I'll get a job."

"Doing what?"

"I'll figure that out."

"Gonna put in an application to the commercial airlines?"

"Hell, no. I'm not suited. Thought about it again when I flew here from Atlanta. Hats off to the pilots who put themselves in charge of five hundred souls on a cross-country flight. I'd sweat through my uniform in the first five minutes."

"I knew it wasn't for me, either, but a commuter flight is manageable. Fewer civilians, more control of conditions. If you don't feel safe taking off, you can just postpone the flight. Everybody understands, at least most of the time."

"That sounds better, but I'm still not ready to—"

"The military gave us structure, and it probably feels weird not to be told what to do every day."

"You've got that right."

"Thanks to you, I was able to make a plan, set up a business that feels more solid every day."

"I'm real happy about that, Cowboy. I love bein' part owner of your business, havin' my name on the logo."

"But you could be a working partner, too! The customers would welcome you with open arms. I get a lot of passengers who are enamored of being flown around by a vet."

"They are?"

"Oh, yeah. We're heroes to them."

Badger glanced at him. "Do you feel like a hero?"

"No, but that's not important. They think of us that way. They admire us because we fought for our country. Some are ex-military themselves. It's a selling point."

"I couldn't work that angle."

"Why not? You were in as long as me."

"But I didn't fight for my country. I wanted to escape, to stop bein' Thaddeus the third. To spit in my daddy's eye. Nothin' noble about that."

Ryker blew out a breath. "And I suppose you did nothing heroic in ten years of flying jets for Uncle Sam?"

"Not that I recall."

"Bullshit. There's Afghanistan, for one."

"Ah, I was showin' off."

"What about those kids in the village? If I remember right, you spent your entire month's paycheck on toys."

"You know I didn't need that damned paycheck. Sorry, you're not gonna convince me I'm a hero. No question about you, though. You went in for the right reasons."

"Then how would you like to be a hero for your old pal Ryker?"

He groaned. "Here it comes. The full-court press."

"I need you here, Badger."

"You don't need me. You only need a fistful of cash to buy that second plane. I can write you a check today. Be happy to do it. Balanced the investments in my trust fund before I came out here and it's healthy as one of your momma's prize chickens."

"Glad to hear it, but I need your flying skills more than your cash."

"Get Stitch. He'll work out perfect."

Ryker blew out a breath. "Yeah, he might. Maybe I don't need you except as an investor."

"There you go."

"But I wouldn't be a good friend if I didn't tell you something."

"What's that?"

"I may not need you to make this business into something great. But I can't shake the feeling that you need me."

He would have loved to have a smartass response to that. He came up empty. He might be as good a pilot as Ryker, maybe even a hair better, but his buddy was miles ahead of him in the wisdom department.

That part about going from a highly structured environment to no structure at all hit home. He'd managed his trust fund well since getting control of it at twenty-five. He'd added a chunk to it while in the military. He'd never have to work another day in his life.

But he desperately needed something to do. He recognized that fact. He just wasn't convinced flying commuter planes out of Eagles Nest was the answer.

To his immense relief, Ryker dropped the subject. Putting the Beechcraft through a couple of barrel rolls helped release some stress. He whooped and hollered like a kid and Ryker joined right in. He did some touch and goes on the runway and the Beechcraft proved as nimble as he'd expected.

Becoming part of Badger Air and flying with Ryker would be fun, no question, but committing to it could end up being a huge mistake.

He didn't have his shit together. He didn't know where he belonged or what he wanted to do with his life. He'd hoped the answer would come to him in the military, but no such luck.

He'd had some vague notion that maybe he'd land in Montana and immediately bond with the place. Not so much. The scenery was spectacular but cold as hell and completely unfamiliar. The town was cute but so different from what he was used to. He had the wrong clothes.

Maybe he did need Ryker and this airline to give him purpose, but his folks would have a coronary if he made that move. Also, if he agreed to join up with Ryker and it all went south, that would destroy their friendship. He wasn't about to take that chance.

_8_

    Walking into the Guzzling Grizzly each Christmas vacation was always a treat for Hayley, especially when she could enjoy lunch with her mom. The place was bustling with customers as usual, and the level of cheerful conversation almost drowned out the sound system's cowboy-themed holiday music.

    The clever decorations likely contributed to everyone's upbeat mood. Last year's had been nice, but they couldn't compare with these. Coiled lariats twined with pine and holly hung at intervals above the polished wooden bar. Christmas lights in the shape of small horseshoes surrounded the mirrored shelving behind the bar and the reflected glow bathed the various bottles lining the shelves.

    A huge wreath made from a wagon wheel dominated one wall of the large room, and a gorgeous blue spruce in the far corner of the bandstand twinkled with white lights and a garland of red and green bandanas. The ornaments were tiny Stetsons, boots and spurs.

    Last year the serviceable wooden tables had been bare, but now they were decked out with red gingham tablecloths and green cloth napkins. In the center of each table was a child-sized boot filled with small branches of pine and holly.

Hayley sat across from her mom and left the menu closed as she continued to look around. "The decorations are fantastic. Way more elaborate than I remember."

"I'd be willing to bet some of this is Nicole's doing."

"Who's Nicole?"

"Bryce McGavin's girlfriend. He owns the bar, now, and he and Nicole perform here together. They're really good."

"Cool! Will they perform Saturday night at the talent show?"

"Oh, I'm sure they will. Everyone will want them to."

"I can see why they'd want to have the place looking extra good." Hayley turned in her chair to make sure she hadn't missed anything. A wreath made of horseshoes, greenery and red bows hung on the far wall and a miniature sleigh filled with wrapped presents sat in a corner.

"Michael probably got into the swing of it, too. I can picture him hanging wreathes and stringing lights."

"I don't know who he is, either."

"Co-owner of the GG. He's bartending today, in fact."

Hayley glanced over her shoulder and got a glimpse of a good-looking cowboy who was busy mixing drinks. He paused to exchange a comment and a smile with a customer sitting at the bar. "He seems to be having fun."

"He's a sweetie. In fact, he was on my list, but I couldn't pin him down." She said it with a perfectly straight face.

Hayley quickly picked up her menu to hide her smile. How lovely that she could afford to be amused, knowing she wouldn't be having a clumsily engineered lunch or dinner with Michael or any other guy this holiday. Her mom seemed to think her efforts were subtle and they never were. *Thank you, Badger.*

As if she'd summoned him, he came through the door, striding purposefully toward their table wearing a mile-wide grin. Ryker followed behind, looking pleased with himself.

She gulped and stared. Somehow she managed to call out a greeting even though the air had left her lungs.

Woo-eee. The man walking toward her bore little resemblance to the one who'd sat in her parents' living room the night before. When he'd left the parsonage, he'd been a handsome Southern boy who'd borrowed a sheepskin jacket to keep warm.

Sometime between then and now, he'd transformed into a fantasy-inducing, breath-stealing heartthrob of a cowboy. Even more amazing, he'd managed to achieve it without looking as if he'd just gone shopping for those duds.

Might partly be the well-worn hat. It could be a hand-me-down courtesy of the McGavins, but damn, did he do it justice—brim low on his forehead, his laughing eyes slightly in shadow. Yum.

The sheepskin jacket and jeans might be new, but if so, the manufacturer had taken pains to make them seem broken in. She didn't have time to check out his boots before he arrived at the table.

He tipped his hat as he glanced at her mother. "Howdy, ma'am." His drawl made the greeting adorably playful.

Hayley was dying to grab him by the lapels and pull him down for a long, hot kiss.

Her mom beamed. "Badger, I almost wouldn't have recognized you except for that gorgeous smile." She glanced past him. "Hello, there, Ryker."

"Ma'am." He tipped his hat in her direction and did the same to Hayley.

"We did a little shoppin' just now." Badger's gaze sought Hayley's before he leaned down and gave her a kiss on the cheek. "Good to see you, darlin'."

"Ditto." Her heartbeat had returned to normal after that dramatic entrance, but the brush of his lips ramped it up again.

"Mind if Ryker and I join you?"

Her mom leaped at the suggestion. "Of course not! We'd love it! What a fun surprise."

"I was hopin' to catch you here. I remembered this was your plan." He unbuttoned his coat and hung it over the back of his chair before sitting down. "Normally in this situation I'd take off my hat, too, but Ryker tells me the Guzzling Grizzly is a place where it's best to leave it on my head."

"Too much danger of losing it or having it stepped on." Ryker draped his jacket over his chair and sat across from Badger. "The former owner even decided his bartenders should wear hats. Thought it gave a more Western look to the place and Bryce decided to—well, speak of the devil, here he comes." Ryker stood as his brother approached. "Hey! Didn't know if you were working today or not."

"Always, bro, always."

"Bryce!" Hayley's mom smiled at him. "I don't think you've met my daughter. This is Hayley."

Bryce tipped his hat. "Pleased to meet you, ma'am." Then he turned toward Badger, who'd left his chair and rounded the table. "And this has gotta be the famous Badger Calhoun."

"In the flesh." Badger shook his hand. "Ryker's told me so much about your music. Can't wait to hear it."

"Thanks for that. Welcome to the GG."

"Great place. I'm impressed with all the Christmas goin' on in your establishment."

"You and me, both. Nicole deserves the credit. I just fetch and carry for her." He surveyed Badger's clothes. "Evidently you got the memo on the Eagles Nest dress code."

"Yep. Ryker gave me a makeover this mornin'."

"Nice job. I see he even contributed his sorry-ass hat to the cause."

"Hey!" Ryker punched his brother lightly on the shoulder. "Don't go maligning my—"

"You mean my hat." Badger tugged the brim a little lower. "You're not gettin' it back. I've been told it lends authenticity to my look."

"That sounds like Mary Jane over at the Western wear shop," Hayley's mom said.

"It was," Ryker said, "but don't worry, ma'am. I informed her he was taken."

"That's good."

Hayley gave Ryker a quick smile. How kind of him to go along with the charade. She had no doubt the clerk was enamored of Badger. Any woman with a pulse would flirt with him in that getup.

"Listen," Bryce said, "since I'm over here and I assume you'd like something to eat, how about telling me what you want?"

Ryker grinned at him. "Now that's what I call top-notch service, having the owner himself take our lunch order."

Bryce laughed. "I'm here to serve, big brother." He turned to the women. "What can I bring you?"

Hayley glanced quickly at the menu. "Last year my burger was terrific. I'll have that, please."

"Make it two, please," her mother said. "And hot herbal tea."

"I'd like coffee." Hayley winked at Badger. "I need the caffeine to maintain my swagger."

Her mother's eyebrows lifted. "You don't have a swagger."

"Inside joke, Mom."

She smiled. "Ah."

After Bryce left with all four orders, Badger sat down and nudged back his hat as if he'd been doing it for years. "Did y'all get your shoppin' done?"

"We did," Hayley said. "The most fun was browsing through the collectibles shop. I found *The Black Stallion Returns* for Luke. We both used to love that series when we were kids."

Badger looked intrigued. "Did you see any Hardy Boys?"

"You know, I think they had a few of those, too."

"I'd like to go in there sometime and check. I was partial to the Hardy Boys but I don't know what happened to my old books. Would be interestin' to read one again."

"Then let's plan to go." She wanted to take him there and help him find a book from his childhood, especially after the conversation with her mother about his parents.

"Great." He reached over and squeezed her hand.

She squeezed back. This was becoming easier and easier, as if they were truly lovers. Crazy.

"I can't get over how different you look, Badger," her mom said. "Like a real cowboy."

"I'm hopin' the horse thinks I'm a real cowboy. Ryker's takin' me out ridin' this afternoon and I want to make a good impression."

"Sounds like fun." Hayley couldn't remember the last time she'd been on a horse. She missed it.

Ryker glanced at her. "Do you ride?"

"Used to, growing up."

"Did she ever," her mom said. "She and Luke desperately wanted horses of their own, but it wasn't feasible. Luckily there was a riding stable nearby."

"Even better, we could get there on our bikes. We mucked out stalls and groomed horses to get extra riding time. Loved it."

"You're welcome to come out and ride with us this afternoon," Ryker said.

"Wow, that would be wonderful! Mom? Do you need me for anything this afternoon?"

"Not a thing." Her mom smiled indulgently.

"Then I'd love to go riding with you two. I'll need to go home and change clothes if that's okay."

"Sure," Ryker said. "Get out there when you can."

"And since you're comin' to dinner," Badger said, "you might as well stay after the ride."

"All right. That's a good idea." She put her napkin in her lap. "How was the flight in the Beechcraft?"

"Awesome. It's a sweet plane. Felt good to be flyin' again. Took a picture of the logo with my phone." He pulled it out of his jacket pocket. "Have you seen it?"

"I don't think so." She peered at his phone and grinned. A cute little badger wore a World War I leather helmet with earflaps. "Adorable. Show my mom."

She looked at the phone. "Very cute! I'll bet that attracts customers."

"It does," Ryker said. "Especially when I talk to people and mention that the airline is named after my Air Force pilot friend. They love knowing that."

Her mom nodded. "Savvy marketing on your part." She turned back to Badger. "So you had fun up there?"

"Big fun." Badger tucked his phone away. "Perfect flying weather. Blue sky, mountains covered with snow. Spectacular."

The sparkle in his eyes told Hayley all she needed to know about what he should be doing with his life. For his sake, she hoped he was seriously considering the idea of working with Ryker.

But that would create an interesting situation. If Badger became a pilot for Badger Air, he'd be living in Eagles Nest next time she came home for Christmas. They might need to talk about how to handle that.

<u>9</u>

After lunch, Badger climbed in Ryker's big black truck. "Why'd you invite Hayley to go ridin'?"

"You don't want her to?" Ryker backed out and pointed the truck in the direction of the ranch.

"I'm happy to have her along, but I sure didn't expect you to be."

"It might be my only chance to ask her how she sees this thing playing out."

"Hey, no, that's not fair. You can't invite her to the ranch so you can grill her."

"I won't. I'll be gentle. But I'm damned curious as to whether you two have an end game in mind."

"I can't speak for her, but it seems simple to me. After the holidays are over and we've both left town, she informs her parents that it didn't work out."

"Will you communicate with them?"

"Will I need to?"

"It would be classy if you sent a note saying how much you appreciated getting to know, them, sorry it didn't work out, blah, blah, blah."

"Did you do that when you and April broke up? You said you were close to her folks."

"Yes, I was close to them, and no, I didn't. I was eighteen and stupid. I wish now I'd done that. They'd treated me like a member of the family and then I just blew off the relationship because I'd broken up with their daughter. I'm lucky they didn't hold it against me when I showed up ten years later."

"I won't be showin' up later, but I see the kindness in that plan. I'll take it under advisement."

"Hm."

"What?"

"Sounds like you've decided against moving here and working with me." The disappointment in his voice was obvious.

"Oh, hey, no! I haven't made that decision. I suppose if I moved here, I would be showin' up later, possibly having contact with her folks. Didn't think of that."

"You had me worried for a minute. I can tell you're not totally sold on the idea, but I'm hoping you'll give it more time to percolate."

"I will, Cowboy. That's only fair after you invited me out here to share in your family's Christmas."

"I wanted you to come. It was mostly so you could meet my family, see the plane and consider whether you wanted to make the move. But I also thought you might want an excuse not to spend the holiday with your folks."

"I most certainly did. And they gave me grief for makin' that choice."

"Par for the course, right? Have they ever approved of your choices?"

"For the first eighteen years I didn't get to make many."

"Not surprising."

"There was this one time when I was ten. We went out to dinner at some five-star restaurant. I don't think it's even there anymore. I decided to be brave and order escargot."

"You thought you'd like snails?"

"I didn't know it was snails. I wanted to prove I could be as sophisticated as they were. It worked. They were impressed as hell until the meal arrived and I refused to eat it. Grossest thing I'd ever seen."

"Can you estimate how long that golden feeling of approval lasted?"

"Probably thirty minutes, tops. It was probably closer to twenty."

"That's it? The only time you can remember them showering praise on you?"

"There might have been others, but that's the only one I remember for sure." He gazed out the window.

"That sucks."

"I know." And their judgment regarding him wasn't likely to change so he'd rather not think about it. "Do you realize how much unoccupied land there is in this area?"

"That's the beauty of Montana. Lots of space."

"And you like that feature."

"Love it. I'm surprised you don't. Think of all the space around you when you're piloting a plane."

"Up there you need it! Otherwise the pilots would constantly be runnin' into one another."

"I personally think you need it at the ground level, too. I couldn't live in Atlanta."

"Yes you could. It's about acclimatin'."

"You think I could change?"

"Sure."

"Then so could you."

"Yeah, but how long would it take? All this empty land freaks me out. When I was drivin' into town last night, surrounded by mostly darkness and a few scattered clusters of lights, I felt like it could be the ocean rollin' around out there."

"I've had that thought. Doesn't bother me but I guess it bothers you."

"I'm just used to lights, buddy. And people. And traffic."

"I understand that. But in Atlanta, you can't get a view of snowy mountains from the air."

"That's a fact, Cowboy. That's a fact."

Ryker folded his arms over the steering wheel and glanced at him. "So tell me. If you didn't know what you wanted to do when you got out, why didn't you stay in?"

"Same reason as you. I heard your voice in my head 'splainin' why you'd decided to leave at the ten-year mark. Younger guys comin' in were a split-second faster. That gap would only get wider as time went on. I didn't want to be the idiot who stayed in too long and got somebody killed because I'd lost my edge."

"Didn't consider a desk job?"

"Just kill me now."

"So here you are."

"Here I am. And I don't know what the hell to do next."

Ryker took a deep breath. "I apologize if I put the pressure on. I want you to throw in with me. Your money's already here, so why not you? But I need to give you time."

"Thanks."

"It would be way simpler if you hadn't gotten yourself tangled up with Hayley."

"Probably. But it's what I do."

Ryker laughed. "At least you admit it." He turned off on the dirt road leading to the ranch. "I can't wait to get you into a Western saddle. You're gonna love it."

An hour later, Badger was acclimating his ass off. Tacking up a horse in Montana didn't bear much resemblance to what he'd been used to at his favorite riding stable in Atlanta.

A Western saddle seemed more appropriate for lounging poolside than riding across the snowy fields of Montana. He used the time before Hayley arrived getting acquainted with Winston and learning how to saddle him. He couldn't get over the weight difference between this saddle and the English ones he was used to.

He settled it on Winston's broad back and the horse grumbled. "Is this extra weight hard on him?"

"I suppose it could be if the saddle doesn't fit right," Ryker said. "We make sure it does. Don't mind his grumbling. He just likes to comment on everything. He likes it if you comment back."

"Is that right, Winston? Are you a talker, buddy? If you are, we'll get along like grits and gravy. I'm a talker, too."

Winston snorted.

"Yeah, I get that reaction a lot. Time to strap you in, Winston, ol' boy." He tightened what he called a girth but Ryker called a cinch. The horse groaned. "I know how it is. I felt the same every time I buckled myself into the F-15. But once you get belted in, you can take off like a rocket."

Ryker chuckled. "Winston's days of taking off like a rocket are behind him. You can get some good speed out of that horse, but you'll have to work up to it."

"Ah, no worries, Winston. We're not plannin' on enterin' the Kentucky Derby, are we? It was just a figure of speech."

Winston snuffled and bobbed his head, making his bridal jingle.

"I like this horse, Cowboy. We're bondin' over here."

"I can tell." Ryker had already saddled his horse, a long-legged bay called Jake. He lifted a saddle onto Strawberry, named for his strawberry roan coat.

"Did he come with the name Winston?"

"Nope." He reached under the roan's belly and grabbed the cinch. "His name was Winner, but after listening to him talk for a month or two, I suggested Winston, after Winston Churchill. I was studying World War II in school."

"I like it. How about Jake?"

"Zane named him after one of his high school friends who moved here from Tennessee. Since Jake is part Tennessee Walker, it seemed appropriate."

"Another Southern boy? Is he still in Eagles Nest?"

"No, but they keep in touch. Jake is Zane's favorite horse, but since he's busy over at the raptor sanctuary, I get to ride Jake. Didn't think about letting you have him since he has that Southern vibe. Want to trade?"

"No, I do not. Me and Winston have made a connection, haven't we, Winnie?"

The horse gave a low chuckle.

"Damn straight we have." Badger scratched underneath Winston's butterscotch and white mane. "Always did want a horse."

"That's something you have in common with Hayley."

"Oh, we have plenty in common." The sound of a car's engine told him she was headed down the ranch road.

"Is that so?"

"Yeah. In a way, I'm sorry that...well, never mind." He gave Winston a pat and walked over to meet Hayley as she parked her rental car next to Ryker's truck.

She climbed out wearing jeans, running shoes and a heavy jacket. She clutched a canvas hat in one hand. "This isn't nearly as fetching as yours, but it's what I could scrounge at the house."

She put it on and tightened the string under her chin. "It's my dad's fishing hat."

"You look cuter'n a speckled pup."

She laughed. "You silver-tongued flatterer, you."

"Where I come from, that's a compliment."

"Where I come from, it isn't." She patted his cheek. "But you meant it to be."

He started to give her a kiss and then remembered Ryker knew the truth about this charade. "Guess I don't have to kiss you."

"Guess not." She held his gaze for a moment before looking away. "This is so exciting for me! I never imagined I'd get to ride on this vacation." She started toward the barn. "Which one do I get?"

"The strawberry roan." He fell into step beside her. "Appropriately named Strawberry." He should have just kissed her.

"He's gorgeous. They all are."

"I'm riding the Paint. That's Winston. And Ryker's riding Jake."

"I can't wait. I might be a little rusty in the beginning, but once I get going I'll be fine."

"At least you're used to that kind of saddle."

"You rode English?"

"Yes, ma'am."

"You should be fine. I think it's probably harder to go from Western to English. Hey, Ryker! Thanks for saddling my horse for me."

"Happy to. Great hat."

"It was either this or a knit one with earflaps, which wouldn't do much to block the sun. Are we ready?"

"Sure are." Ryker gestured to the horse he'd just saddled. "This is Strawberry."

"So Badger said. I can't thank you enough for inviting me."

"You're most welcome. Need a hand up?"

"No, thanks. I've got it." She accepted the reins and mounted in one fluid motion. "Ahhh. I love seeing the world from the back of a horse."

"Me, too, Hayley." Ryker smiled up at her. "The only thing better is seeing it from the cockpit of a plane."

"I couldn't say since I've never done that."

"You should try it sometime."

Badger was amused by Ryker's quick turnaround. After his initial blustery reaction to this caper, he was charmed by Hayley's zest for life. He wasn't the only one.

He looked at Badger. "Okay, flyboy. Mount up."

"Aye, aye, cap'n." He swung into the saddle and Winston groaned again. "Sorry, Winnie. I shouldn't have had the chocolate cake for dessert."

"But wasn't it great?" Hayley neck-reined Strawberry away from the hitching rail. "I have to have it every Christmas. Which way, Ryker?"

"I thought we'd take the trail Zane uses when he's releasing one of his raptors. It's real pretty."

"Then lead on." She glanced at Badger. "Do you want to fall in behind him? After all, this was supposed to be a ride for you two. That way you can talk. I'll just meander along behind and enjoy the scenery."

He shook his head. "Ladies first."

"Should have known you'd insist on that. By the way, you look great on that horse."

"Winston would make anyone look great. He's a showy animal."

"He is, but—"

"You two coming or not?" Ryker turned in the saddle. "We're burning daylight."

"On our way, Cowboy!" Badger winked at her. "We'll continue this discussion later."

Her blue eyes sparkled and her cheeks turned pink. "Counting on it."

Yeah, he absolutely should have kissed her a while ago. Surely he'd have another opportunity. If not, he'd make one.

10

Hayley was in her element. Not only was she on horseback, but she was riding through a snow-covered landscape between two handsome cowboys. The scenery was primo. The mountains and evergreen forest views were nice, too.

She only wished Badger's manners hadn't dictated that he had to let her go ahead of him. She wouldn't have minded following him down the trail and feasting her gaze on the fantasy he'd turned into. He'd impressed her when he'd walked into the Guzzling Grizzly, but when he'd mounted that beautiful Paint with such ease, she'd nearly swooned.

The path through the snow had been trampled by horses but clearly the previous riders had gone single file. Conversation would involve too much twisting in the saddle. Better to stay quiet. The peaceful silence of the wide meadow was broken only by the squeak of leather and the steady clop of hooves.

Strawberry was a perfect gentleman. She told him so and patted his silky neck. His ears flicked backward to pick up her soft murmurs.

Behind her, Badger seemed to be having a conversation with Winston. She couldn't make out what he was saying, but Winston was noisier than either of the other horses. His snuffles, snorts and groans became funny after a while.

About thirty yards ahead of them, four white-tailed deer—a buck and three does—leaped from the shelter of the trees and bounded across the meadow. Ryker raised his hand and pulled Jake to a halt.

Hayley followed suit.

When the small band had disappeared into the forest on the other side of the meadow, Ryker swiveled in his saddle. "They could be running from a predator. If so, I don't want it to startle the horses."

"Good call." Hayley stood in her stirrups and stretched. "What an amazing vista, Ryker."

"You have vistas near you, too."

"I do, but I get involved in work and forget to take advantage of the beauty outside. Thank you for reminding me how much I need this."

"I was just telling Badger that we all do. He's partial to lights and traffic."

She twisted in her saddle. "Lights and traffic instead of this?"

"I'm just used to a big city. You said you are, too."

"I did say that, but when you're in the heart of a city, you have to deliberately plan to get out in nature. It's easy to forget to do it. Here, you can't forget. It's right out your back door."

"Hear that, Badger? Thanks for helping me make my case, Hayley."

"It's not an easy decision, though," she said. "I love my job."

"What is your job? I don't think Badger ever said."

"I work in elder care. My agency helps seniors in the Denver area stay happy and healthy."

"Worthy cause."

"Thanks. I think so. Very satisfying. We've made a lot of progress."

"Then I can see why you'd want to keep at it." Ryker surveyed the meadow. "Since there's no sign of a predator, let's move on. We're almost there." He clucked to Jake and started down the trail again.

Hayley turned to glance back at Badger. "What are you saying to Winston? It sounds like you two are talking to each other."

"We are. Ryker told me Winston appreciates a good conversation, so I want him to enjoy the experience today."

"What are you talking about?"

He grinned. "We're discussin' how nice you look ridin' ahead of us."

"You are not."

"Yes, ma'am, we are."

"Me? In this old jacket and fishing hat?"

"Winston and I have decided that you transcend the outfit."

"Oh, you have, have you?" Her heart beat faster. "Just so you know, that comment is way more effective than telling me I'm cuter than a speckled pup."

"Is it effective enough that it might earn me a kiss later on?"

"That's a distinct possibility."

"Hey, guys!" Ryker motioned them forward. "Move 'em out! We don't have all day, you know."

Badger chuckled. "That boy needs to learn how to relax. Most things in life benefit from a leisurely pace."

"I take it you know that from personal experience?"

"Yes, ma'am." He gave her a lazy smile. "I surely do."

"Guys!"

"Coming, Ryker!" Hayley faced forward and nudged Strawberry into a trot. Badger might not have meant his comment to be sexual, but since he'd brought up the subject of kissing, she'd taken it that way.

She spent the rest of the ride turning herself on at the prospect of being alone with him again. But that might not happen anytime soon.

Ryker had been kind enough to be their trail guide and they couldn't have taken such a spectacular ride without him. She was grateful, but now she hoped he had somewhere else to be. Turned out her wish was granted.

As they rode up to the barn, Ryker pulled out his phone and checked the time. "Yikes. We're later than I thought. I'm supposed to pick up April at home and bring her back here for dinner. Would you guys be okay grooming the horses while I go get her?"

"Absolutely." Hayley's imagination kicked in. This could be the private moment she'd hoped for. "Just show me where the grooming supplies are and where the saddles and blankets go. I'm a good hand."

"And I'm good at following directions," Badger said.

"All right." Ryker dismounted. "Thanks."

Hayley followed him into the tack room to get her instructions, but she barely needed any. The routine was similar to what she'd done before at the riding stable.

As he started out the door, she put a hand on his sleeve. "Before you leave, does April know the real story with Badger and me?"

"No." Ryker glanced at his buddy standing nearby. "And Badger is aware that I *hate* keeping secrets from the woman I love."

"I know you do," Badger said quietly. "I surely appreciate that you're doin' it."

"Me, too," Hayley said. "I didn't stop to think how many people this scheme could affect."

Ryker sighed. "Now that I know you a little better, I'm more willing to do this for you. You're a nice person, Hayley. I just hope this doesn't blow up in your face. Or Badger's."

"It won't, Cowboy." Badger clapped him on the shoulder. "Now go get April."

The grooming didn't take long. Hayley hadn't expected it to, and every minute saved was time alone with Badger. A quick call to Kendra confirmed which horse went in which stall.

Winston's was the farthest from the door and Badger led him down there while she waited.

After he closed the stall door, he started back down the aisle with long, purposeful strides.

Her heart began to pound. "You look like a man on a mission."

"I am." He grabbed her hand and tugged her down the aisle. "I'm kissin' you, Hayley Bennett."

"Glad to hear it, but where are we going?"

"Tack room."

"Why?"

"More private, just in case."

"In case?"

"We get carried away."

"Oh." Heat swept through her, leaving her quivering.

He pulled her inside the tack room, slid the door closed and laid his hat on a shelf. "I've been dreamin' about this all day." Gently he loosened the string under her chin, removed her hat, and set it next to his.

"But don't let me forget my—"

"I won't let you forget it, darlin'." He framed her face in both hands and tilted it up to his. He searched her gaze. "Now we get to find out if last night's kiss was a fluke."

She could barely breathe. He was so incredibly gorgeous. She'd never anticipated a kiss this much. "Do you...think it was?"

"No."

"Me, either." She closed her eyes as his mouth settled over hers. *Heaven.* Perfect fit. She sank against him as he coaxed her jaw open and boldly claimed her with his tongue. She moaned and clutched the back of his head.

This was good, very good, but it wasn't enough. He kissed with a sensuality that left her dizzy and aching. Oh, the promises he made with that tongue! She wanted him to fulfill all of them. *Now.*

As he continued to ravish her with his talented mouth, he worked her out of her jacket and unfastened her shirt. Lord help her, she aided and abetted. She longed for his touch.

Her shirt hit the floor, joining her fallen jacket. Her bra followed. Panting, he drew back and gazed at her with heavy-lidded eyes. "I knew you would look like this, feel like this." Cradling her breasts in his cupped hands, he brushed his thumbs over her aching nipples.

She covered his hands with hers and closed her eyes. "I want—"

"So do I, darlin'." His voice was strained. "I didn't count on this."

"Me, either." She opened her eyes and gazed into his. "I never imagined that we'd be so, so—"

"Hot for each other?" Sliding his hands to the small of her back, he pulled her closer.

"Yeah." She flattened her palms against his chest and absorbed the rapid beat of his heart.

"And everybody but Ryker thinks we've already..."

"I know, but we haven't." She looked into his eyes. Her frustration was reflected back to her. "Is that ridiculous or what?"

"But if we could find a way..." He dragged in a shaky breath. "No one would question it."

"What way could there possibly be?"

He swallowed. "Don't know. But if I find one, will you..."

"Yes! But it's unlikely. We have chaperones everywhere and—"

"Hey, guys and gals! Who's ready for dinner?" The hearty question from right outside the door was followed by Winston's loud whinny.

Badger leaned down and murmured in her ear. "This is why we need a hidey-hole."

She nodded and worked to steady her breathing. His warm breath tickling her ear didn't help.

"Probably Cody. Sounds like him."

"Maybe we should just stay here and be quiet."

"Makes no sense. Why would we hide?"

"You're right."

"Come out when you're ready." He gave her a soft kiss, put on his hat and left the tack room, closing the door firmly behind him.

Snatching her shirt and bra from the floor, she put them on. She fastened the buttons with shaking hands. Sexual frustration combined with an unexpected interruption had loaded her up with adrenalin. Last of all she put on her jacket and grabbed her dad's fishing hat from the shelf where Badger had laid it.

Badger and Cody, if that's who it was, were talking just outside the door. She heard laughter. Being discovered was a good thing for the tall tale she and Badger had cooked up. It was turning out to be a very convincing story. Just so she didn't start believing it.

_11_

Badger hadn't been interrupted while making out with a woman in a long, long time, not since Atlanta's finest had caught him with his pants down in the back seat of Eileen Stanley's BMW.

He had his pants on this time, but when he'd come out of the tack room, he hadn't been exactly presentable.

Sure enough, it had been Cody who'd arrived to feed the horses. His startled reaction at seeing Badger had changed to speculation and then he'd started laughing. "Hey, sorry."

"No problem." Badger couldn't help laughing, too. It was a funny situation. "The horses need to be fed."

"True, but you and Hayley must be a little frustrated with this setup."

"You could say that."

"I mean, with her staying at the parsonage and you sleeping here, I wondered what you planned to do about the issue."

"Clearly we haven't solved it or we wouldn't be makin' out in the tack room."

"I had a similar problem with Faith. She was at her dad's house and I was here."

"What'd you do about it?"

"Well, it was June, for one thing."

"Oh. You could sneak off in the bushes."

"That was her plan but I wasn't crazy about it. I set up a bed inside my camper shell."

"Wasn't that kind of obvious?"

"Not really. I was planning for my upcoming road trip, so it looked like preparations for my journey. But mostly it was so Faith and I could get horizontal in comfort. The ground is not optimal."

"And now it's really out of the question."

"Yeah." Cody laughed. "I'd hate to think what would happen if you tried it in the snow."

"Shrinkage would happen, that's what."

Cody grinned. "Yep. Not the way to impress your lady."

"Hauling her into the tack room isn't exactly smooth, either. Is there a hotel around here? Or a B&B?"

"There is. Let me—oh, hey, there." He turned as Hayley came out, her cheeks flushed. "I'm trying to remember if we've ever officially met."

"I don't think so. These aren't the circumstances I would have chosen for our first meeting, either."

"Don't give it another thought." He stuck out his hand. "Cody McGavin at your service, ma'am."

"Hayley Bennett." She shook his hand.

Winston chose that moment to let out a piercing whinny.

Cody laughed. "There's the dinner bell! You two want to help feed? I could use a hand. Faith's up at the house cooking with Mom. We'll eat well tonight."

"I'm sure. And I'd love to help feed."

"Me, too," Hayley said.

"Then let's fetch us some gloves." Cody walked into the tack room. Later, as they were delivering hay flakes loaded into a wheelbarrow, he had a moment when Hayley wasn't within earshot. "That place that might work?"

"Yeah?"

"I'll get you the info tonight."

"Great. Thanks."

* * *

The massive dinner table piled with food and the joking that went on during the meal reminded Badger of nights in the mess hall, only with more women. He'd served with female pilots, even dated a couple, but they weren't in the majority.

Tonight they outnumbered the guys by two. Neither Kendra nor Aunt Jo had a sweetheart. Cowboy had told him the stories—Aunt Jo had divorced her cheating husband years ago. Kendra's Air Force pilot husband had died young, ironically not in the service but at home from an aneurism. Clearly both women were strong enough to make it on their own.

But the others gathered around the table seemed able to take care of themselves, too. Not a shrinking violet in the bunch. Hayley, who sat on his left, fit right in.

He'd been impressed with Faith earlier, but this was his first introduction to Mandy and Zane. Mandy was a powerhouse who ran her own fashion business with one hand and helped Zane's Raptor Rise operation with the other.

Zane recounted the latest rescue of a male bald eagle who had become tangled in the string from a Mylar balloon. "Fortunately we discovered him before he'd hurt himself. He'll be fine." He turned to Badger. "How soon can you come over for a tour of the facility?"

"How's tomorrow afternoon?"

"Great." Zane looked at Hayley. "You're welcome to come, too."

"I'd love to, but I promised to bake Christmas cookies with my mom. It's a yearly tradition."

"Wouldn't want to mess with that," Badger said. "What if I go tomorrow and then we can go over together after Christmas?"

"Perfect."

"You'll be blown away by the tour." Bryce's girlfriend Nicole had bright red hair and the enthusiastic attitude to go with it. "That place is amazing."

"I'll bet. I've been wantin' to see it ever since I saw some pictures y'all sent over. And there was a video of a golden eagle release, too."

"I took that." Aunt Jo looked proud of herself. "I'll never forget the experience."

"I'm sure I wouldn't, either." Badger glanced at Zane. "Any releases scheduled in the next few days?"

"Sorry. Not for another month or so."

"Stick around and you can see one," Ryker said.

Olivia, Trevor's girlfriend and the McGavin family accountant, spoke up. "Don't forget I want to go on the January release."

"I've got you down." Zane looked over at Badger, his gaze steady. "Want to reserve a spot? They're going fast."

"Hey, boys." Kendra tapped her fork against her glass. "No hard sell, especially at the table. We all hope he'll choose to live here. Let's leave it at that."

Cody grinned at Ryker. "Yeah, stop *badgering* the poor guy."

Everybody groaned, but Kendra's edict held. The subject was dropped.

April had made sure to sit on his right, and he'd enjoyed getting to know her. She was a little thing, and friendly as all get out. Clearly her cheerful personality softened Ryker's drill sergeant tendencies. Seated on April's other side, Ryker relaxed in his chair and sipped a beer while watching her with an adoring gaze.

"What was Ryker like in the Air Force?" she asked as the meal wound down. "You're the only one here who can tell us."

"You want the truth?"

"That's why I'm asking."

"He was a pain in the ass."

Her brown eyes sparkled with mischief. "Funny, he says the same about you."

Badger looked at Ryker over the top of April's head. "You do?"

Ryker shrugged. "I call 'em like I see 'em."

"Okay, tell me this." April tucked her napkin next to her plate. "Who's the better pilot?"

"I am," they said together.

She laughed. "Probably could have predicted that. Okay, one more question, Badger. Did he ever talk about me?"

Ryker put down his beer. "Answer that and you're a dead man."

Badger grinned at him. "Only when he was drunk."

Ryker's eyes narrowed.

"And what did he talk about?"

"Sorry, ma'am." He held Ryker's gaze. "I'm not at liberty to say."

"Well done, Badger." Kendra pushed back her chair and stood. "It looks like we've avoided bloodshed. Who's ready for dessert?"

"Hot damn." Zane got up, too. "We finally get to eat the Yule log you've been raving about."

"We're eating a Yule log?" Badger was confused. "Isn't that what you burn?"

"That's what I thought, too," Ryker said. "I could swear I saw a birch log in the fireplace, like always."

"And another one in the fridge," Cody said.

"Actually I got two." Kendra started gathering plates and everyone else stood to do the same. "I wanted plenty to go around."

As they all carried dishes and food into the kitchen, Badger turned to Hayley. "Does your family burn a Yule log for the twenty-first?"

"No fireplace."

"Oh, right. What about this other one that's for dessert?"

"I've never heard of it, but it sounds cool."

"And tastes even better." Kendra pulled two large bakery boxes out of the refrigerator and set them on the counter. When she lifted the lids, everyone gathered around to admire what looked like two branched logs frosted with chocolate and decorated with molded sugar poinsettias and tiny mushrooms.

Badger whistled under his breath. "Those are a work of art."

"They are." Hayley was wedged in next to him. "Seems a shame to cut into them."

Crowded in with Ryker's family and Hayley pressed against his side, Badger had trouble separating fantasy from reality. If he had to choose right now, he'd choose the fantasy of being madly in love with Hayley.

"Oh, you'll want to cut into them," Mandy said. "It's delicious, a thin layer of chocolate cake rolled up with mocha chocolate mousse inside. And buttercream frosting textured to look like bark. I ate one of the samples Abigail was passing out last week. Take a picture if you want to save it for posterity."

"I'll take a picture to show my folks." Hayley jostled Badger as she pulled out her phone. "I'm going to suggest this for next year."

He could have moved a little to give her more room, but he liked being mashed together so he held his position.

"Okay, you've all seen it," Kendra said. "Who wants to help serve? Not you, Trevor. You're in charge of the fireplace."

Several people offered to help, including Hayley, who said she'd waitressed her way through college.

Kendra smiled at her. "Then we'd be grateful to have you. Jo and I never waitressed a day in our lives."

"I'll help, too," Badger said. "I've never been a waiter, but if I can juggle empty plates I can probably manage full ones."

"Juggling practice!" Ryker snapped his fingers. "We should practice after we finish dessert. I stashed a box of red and green thrift-store plates in my old bedroom. Mom, if you don't need me, I'll go get 'em for later."

"Looks like we have plenty of hands on deck, son. Go ahead."

"I'll help serve," Cody said. "But I need a quick minute with Badger." He motioned him back into the dining room and took out his phone. "Get your phone, buddy."

Badger took his out of his pocket.

"Here you go." Cody showed Badger his screen. "The Nesting Place B&B. I'm texting you the number."

"Excellent. Thanks, Cody." He couldn't duck out now, but he'd find a moment during the evening. The way things were going with Hayley, he needed to find a place where they could deal with their lust or one of them was liable to go up in flames before this vacation was over.

_12_

What a wonderful evening. Hayley had loved it all—the traditions, the teasing, the room filled with laughter. And singing. Bryce and Nicole had brought their guitars and had played any Christmas carol thrown at them.

Badger, Ryker and Cody put on a brief juggling demonstration. They were way better at it than Hayley had expected. April told her Ryker was a genius at hand-eye coordination, but she admitted Badger might be his equal. Cody was the team's weak link, but he didn't seem to care. He was endearingly good-natured about it.

The magic of Christmas was alive and well at Wild Creek Ranch. She didn't want to leave, but she didn't share a room down the hall with Badger. The birch Yule log in the fireplace had been reduced to hot coals by the time she got to her feet and announced she should go home.

That prompted a touching flurry of hugs and suggestions that she should consider moving to Eagles Nest.

"Montana has all sorts of elder care programs," Zane said. "We could put you to work, no problem."

"You could be a roving consultant," April said. "Ryker could fly you all over the state, right, cowboy?"

Badger looked at her. "You call him Cowboy, too? I thought it was only me and the guys in our squadron."

April smiled at him. "I've called him that forever, but it's not like his handle or anything. Out here, if you happen to be dealing with a guy who can ride and rope, you might call him cowboy for the heck of it. I think you gave Ryker an actual name, with a capital C."

"Yes, ma'am. He was the only one who got that label. Just like I was the only one who was called Badger."

"And who gave you that name?"

Hayley was glad April had asked the question. She'd wanted to, but their relationship was so new that she'd hesitated.

"My first year in the service there was a guy in my squadron who liked matchin' people with their...I forget what he called it."

"Spirit animals?"

"That's it. He decided that a badger worked for me because I walk my own path at my own pace. That's the general idea, anyway."

April smiled. "That's awesome. Do you?"

Badger gazed at her. "Mostly."

"Good." April gave him a hug. "I'm glad to have finally met you, Badger. And for the record, I admire you for keeping Ryker's secrets. I didn't expect you to crack."

"I wasn't bein' noble, ma'am. As you observed, he threatened to kill me."

"You and I both know he'd rather cut out his heart than hurt you."

Ryker wrapped an arm around her waist. "Gee, thanks. You just ruined my last chance to intimidate this joker. From now on, he'll ride roughshod over me."

She laughed. "Like anyone could ride roughshod over you."

"Except you." He drew her against his side.

"That's the truth. She's got your number, Cowboy." Badger captured Hayley's hand in his. "Now if y'all will excuse me, I'll walk this lady to her car." He helped her on with her coat.

As they went out the front door, people called out *Merry Christmas* and *call me*. She'd given her phone number to most of the women. She'd be in Eagles Nest through New Year's, so coffee dates were a definite possibility.

"They like you," Badger said as they walked across the porch and down the steps, his arm draped across her shoulder.

"I like them."

"It seemed like you made a connection with everyone, especially the women."

"I did. But I need to be realistic. You're Ryker's pal from the military. If I dump you after the vacation, I doubt they'll want to have anything to do with me."

"Then don't dump me."

Her breathing picked up speed. She stopped walking and turned, dislodging his arm. Her breath made little puffs of fog in the still air, broadcasting her agitation. "But...but I thought we'd agreed to—"

"Easy, darlin'. Don't panic." He smiled down at her. "We'll still break up."

"Oh." She swallowed. "You had me worried for a minute."

"Didn't mean to scare you. I'm not deviatin' from the plan. Just refinin' it. We'll break up, but it doesn't have to be acrimonious."

His pre-law education was showing. But she wasn't supposed to know about that. "You're right. We've set it up that we haven't spent a lot of time together. It would be logical that we'd find some issue we hadn't anticipated."

"Why does it have to be an issue? Why can't we just go our separate ways?"

"Because we've sold this as a love match. Everybody thinks we're crazy about each other, so we need to butt heads over something."

He nudged back his hat. "I'm a pretty easy goin' guy. Not the buttin' heads type. Can't we just tell everybody it didn't work out?"

"You can get away with that sometimes, but your nearest and dearest will think you're hiding your pain."

"Ryker won't."

"My mom and dad will, though, and Kendra might. When a couple's madly in love, it doesn't end with a handshake. There's anguish and misery."

"Then I guess I've never been madly in love."

"You've never suffered when you split with someone?"

He shrugged. "No, ma'am. Just figured it wasn't meant to be and moved on. Have you suffered?"

"Only one time to the point of long crying jags, and that was when I was in college. I was madly in love and so was he, with me and three other women. He said he needed all of us for different reasons."

"Bastard." He touched her cheek. "I'm sorry. Wish I could break his nose for you."

She laughed. "No worries. I broke it."

"Whoa! Well done, you. Did you punch him?"

"Nope. Whacked him in the face with my sociology textbook. Good thing some classes still used actual books then. I wouldn't have risked my laptop. Anyway, no one wondered why we called it quits."

"I get that. Listen, are you cold? Because I'm—"

"I'm freezing."

"Then how about continuin' this conversation in your car? And turnin' on the heater?"

"That's brilliant." She fished out her keys and started for the rental sedan. "So what else could we disagree on? Religion?"

"I believe in live and let live."

"Politics?"

"People split up over that?"

"Sometimes."

"I wouldn't."

"You sure are easy to get along with, Badger." She clicked open the locks.

He beat her to the door handle and opened it for her. "I'm just a good ol' Southern boy. Nothin' special."

"Now there's something we could argue about." She slid behind the wheel.

"I would purely enjoy listenin' to you argue the case for me bein' exceptional. We could do that all day." He closed her door and walked around the back of the car.

Oh, yeah. His pricy education was sticking out all over him. She started the car and turned on the heater.

When Badger climbed in the back seat instead of the front, she turned. "What the..." But his grin said it all. "I assume you want to do more than talk."

"Yes, ma'am." He unbuttoned his coat and reached over the console to lay his hat brim-side up on the passenger seat.

"What if someone comes along?"

"They'll see a car with the motor running and the windows steamed up."

"How do you know? You've never made out in cold country."

"But I saw *Titanic.* There's that scene where the couple goes into a car being transported and—"

"We're not doing that."

"No, we're not." He shrugged out of his coat. "I'm just plannin' on kissin' you. But I can't accomplish that unless you come on back here."

"We haven't finished our discussion."

"We'll multi-task."

"Okay." She set the emergency brake and opened the door. "What about kids?" Once outside, she quickly took off her parka and tossed it on the seat.

"I promise we won't be makin' any of those tonight."

"I meant what about kids as a subject we can't agree on? Do you want any?" She closed the driver's door as he leaned across and opened the back one.

"I haven't given it much thought."

She climbed in and closed it behind her. "Perfect. I do want at least one and maybe two."

"Sounds nice." He pulled her close.

"You can be the one who doesn't want—"

"Hold that thought. I have some kissin' to do." His mouth found hers. Heavenly days, did he know how to do this.

He teased, he sipped and then he took command. He had the most seductive tongue of any man she'd ever kissed. When he finally drew back, her panties were damp and her hands were inside his shirt. She must have unfastened the snaps.

Oh, and climbed over to his side of the car, too. She was straddling him, sitting on his muscled thighs while she clutched his shoulders for support. If she scooted forward, she'd do him serious injury.

But she wasn't going anywhere. His grip on her ass was so tight she wouldn't be surprised if the denim began fraying.

"Oh, darlin'." He gulped for air. "You're torturin' this poor boy."

"And myself." Her heart beat so fast she was dizzy. "But I can't help it." Then she was kissing him again, because she couldn't be this close and not feel those supple lips against hers. She wanted more from him, so much more...

He groaned and cradled her face in both hands before leaning back, putting a sliver of space between them. "We have to...have to... stop." His harsh breathing matched her own.

"I know!" She sounded like a crazy person. "What are we going to do?"

He took a long shaky breath and swallowed. "I have a plan." He sucked in more air. "Can I take you to breakfast?"

"Now?"

"In the mornin'. Can you do that?"

"Breakfast." It seemed so far away. She cleared her throat. "I guess. Then what?"

"Tell you in the mornin'." His chest heaved and he opened the door. "I need a short walk before I can say a proper goodbye."

"To where?"

"Nearest snowbank. Gonna roll in it."

_**13**_

A snowbank wasn't necessary, after all, but Badger had thought so until he'd left Hayley in the car and walked coatless out into the night. That woman was dynamite. But after five minutes strolling around the parking area, his jeans no longer threatened to turn him into a eunuch.

He'd thought about telling Hayley the solution he'd come up with. He still could when he went back to the car. But if she knew, she might act different with her momma, and he didn't want her momma to know about this. Not yet, anyway.

There was a slim, very slim possibility that he and Hayley wouldn't be compatible in bed. He doubted it, but no two people could ever be sure they'd get along between the sheets, even if the make-out sessions were hotter than an Atlanta sidewalk in July.

Consequently, he'd decided to surprise her with this setup and see if it worked out. If so, it wouldn't matter who knew about it. If their morning interlude was less than wonderful, then it could be one more secret to keep from the rest of the world.

By the time he returned to the car, she was in the driver's seat with the defroster going and he was eager to have his coat and hat back.

She handed them out the window. "Better?"

"Yes, ma'am. How're you doin'?"

"Not too bad." She left the window down and gazed up at him. "Breakfast, huh?"

"That's right."

"You didn't say what time."

He'd worked that out earlier, thank God. He'd checked on his phone and Pills and Pop, the town's nostalgic little drugstore, opened at eight because of the holidays. "How about eight-fifteen?"

"Why not just make it eight?"

"Eight-fifteen sounds more interestin'."

"You have something up your sleeve, don't you?"

"Who, me?"

"You have that same expression you had when we were on the plane and you suggested this caper. What's going on?"

"It's a surprise." His feet and hands were getting cold. Shoving his hands in his pockets, he stamped his feet.

"Will I like it?"

"I hope so."

"Okay, if you're not going to tell me—"

"I'm not."

"Then I'll head home."

He leaned down and gave her a quick kiss. "See you at eight-fifteen." He backed away from the car and waited until she was on her way down the ranch road before he went in the house.

Upon his return to the living room, everyone teased him about the long goodbye. Everybody but Ryker, who looked as if he'd like to have a private conversation. But no opportunities presented themselves and Badger didn't try to make one.

Ryker probably only wanted to lecture him about getting deeper into something he shouldn't have started in the first place. But what was he supposed to do? Hayley wanted this as much as he did, and he wasn't about to disappoint the lady.

The late night was a blessing, because he was still fighting jet lag. Between all the activity that day and staying up longer, he slept later. The night before, he'd told Kendra he'd be taking Hayley to breakfast and had received permission to borrow her truck.

After showering and dressing, he had time to head down to the stable, locate Jim and ask about the sleigh ride schedule. Luckily Jim had an opening at eleven.

"Then I'd surely appreciate it if I could have that slot," Badger said. "I'd like to treat Hayley to a sleigh ride."

"You've got it." Jim gave him a warm smile. "What a nice idea."

"I think she'll like it." The sleigh ride was an add-on so that if Hayley needed to tell her momma later what the surprise had been, she could mention the sleigh ride. He thought she might appreciate having that be the reason their breakfast ended up taking all morning.

In his eagerness to get this show on the road, he ended up parked in front of Pills and Pop a few minutes before it opened. He climbed out of the truck and paced up and down the sidewalk in front of the store.

Two display windows had been set up like Christmas windows of old, with an electric train circling in one, complete with cotton snow, a tunnel, and a little village gathered around it. The other window had dolls, toy trucks, a box of magic tricks, a little red wagon and several teddy bears.

Christmas had never been like this for him. He'd only seen it in movies. His childhood holidays had been spent in some exotic place, either a tropical paradise or a skiing destination.

He couldn't remember any of his gifts. They were usually something his parents bought once they arrived, a toy a local kid might love but not the kind of thing an American kid would long for. His parents were in Biarritz right now. They'd been disappointed that he'd chosen Eagles Nest over a resort town in France.

The lock on the drugstore's front door clicked and a woman opened it. The lines in her face told him she was at least eighty. But the rest of her looked forty years younger. Her hair was colored a soft brown and carefully styled. Her outfit was fashionable and her four-inch heels showed off slim calves and ankles.

Her gaze was direct. "Young man, you obviously are desperate to get in here. It's still two minutes before we open, but I'll let you in early because it's the holidays."

"Yes, ma'am. Thank you, ma'am." He tipped his hat.

Her gaze softened. "You're Southern."

"Yes, ma'am. Georgia born and bred."

"My first husband was Southern. He wasn't worth a plugged nickel but that accent was divine in bed."

He swallowed a laugh. She didn't look as if she'd meant it as a joke, just a statement of fact.

"What can I help you find, young man?"

"Well, ma'am, I need a certain item before I meet a beautiful young lady this mornin'."

"You mean a gift?"

"I wouldn't say it's exactly a gift. More like a necessity for a shared event."

"Are you coming in here at eight in the morning to buy *condoms*?" She had a voice that could carry.

He stepped closer and lowered his in hopes she'd be more discreet. "I am."

No such luck. She looked him up and down. "If that don't beat all. I've had customers come in here in the middle of the day looking for that item, planning for a future rendezvous."

"Yes, ma'am."

"And a greater percentage come in during the evening hours because they didn't plan ahead."

"Yes, ma'am."

"I can't say I've ever had someone pacing outside the store waiting to buy condoms at this hour. That's a first."

"Yes, ma'am." He pictured this story going all over town. Even worse, it didn't fit the scenario that he and Hayley had concocted. If they were almost engaged, he'd have brought this item with him to Eagles Nest. He wouldn't be hanging outside the local drugstore so he could buy it the minute it opened.

She laid a hand on his arm. "You look concerned."

"I am, a little, because—"

"Don't be." She took his arm and guided him over to the condom display. "Choose what you need. I won't ask questions. And you won't hear this gossip anywhere in town."

"I won't?"

"It's not my style." She held out her hand. "Ellie Mae Stockton, at your service."

He shook her hand. "Pleased to meet you, ma'am. I'm Badger Calhoun."

"Badger! Are you Ryker McGavin's Air Force friend?"

"Yes, ma'am."

"How long have you been in town?"

"I got here Wednesday afternoon."

"And this is only Friday morning. You're a fast worker, Badger Calhoun."

"Well, you see, I—"

"No explanation necessary. I know from personal experience that a Southern accent can convince a girl to ditch her panties." She patted his arm. "Thirty years ago, I would have been just as willing as whoever you're buying these for. She's a lucky lady. Now get what you need. Clearly you're in a hurry."

"Yes, ma'am."

"Then let's not keep her waiting. I'll meet you at the cash register." She bustled off.

He paid for the condoms and left the store, but not before he glanced at the old-fashioned soda fountain. It wasn't open for business at this hour and might not be as popular in the winter months.

Hayley might not come here in the summer. But if she did, if circumstances were such that they were both here, he'd want to invite her to Pills and Pop for hot fudge sundaes, or milkshakes, or root beer floats.

Despite what he'd said to Ryker about needing a city that was open for business 24/7, he was developing a fondness for this little town. A clerk in a chain drugstore wouldn't have taken a personal interest in his need for condoms at eight in the morning.

Yesterday he would have said he preferred the impersonal nature of buying condoms in a big city. The purchase was nobody's business. Today he'd met Ellie Mae Stockton, who'd told him his accent was special and his girlfriend was a lucky lady. That interaction had changed his preference. Being an anonymous customer didn't deliver the biggest bang for the buck.

In fact, buying this package of condoms, a feat he'd had to engineer because he wasn't in Atlanta, had been a hundred times more satisfying and even significant than if he'd dashed into a drugstore chain. There he would have grabbed something off the rack, paid for it and hurried out of the store.

Before he left the parking space, he opened the package and tucked two condoms in his jeans pocket. He might not need both. If Hayley rejected the entire program, he wouldn't need any.

He parked in the parsonage driveway. Hayley's rental was parked in the street, probably so she wouldn't block the drive when either of her parents needed to come out. But he wouldn't be here long so he'd take a chance.

Ringing the doorbell should have been a cinch after breaking the ice the night before, but this time he had two condoms burning a hole in his pocket. It wasn't the first instance he'd walked into a girl's parents' house packing raincoats, but it might be the first time he'd done it before nine in the morning.

Hayley greeted him at the door looking festive in a bright green sweater and jeans. "Hey, you." She grabbed him by the lapels of his sheepskin coat and pulled him into a quick kiss.

"Hayley, is that Badger?"

"Yeah, Mom!" She let go of his coat and smoothed the lapels back in place.

He grinned at her. "Nice welcome."

"I missed you. I—"

"Will you ask him to come talk to me for a minute? I have a question about dinner tonight."

"Sure!" She turned back to him. "You don't have any food allergies, do you?"

"Nothing that I know of."

"That's what I thought, but I'd hate to be wrong and have you swell up like a balloon at dinner."

"My swelling issue has nothing to do with allergies."

"You're a bad boy." She smirked and gave him a little push toward the kitchen.

Taking off his hat, he walked through the quiet living room and into the kitchen.

Virginia had a recipe book open on the counter and was stirring ingredients into a large bowl. She glanced up. "Hi, Badger. Once I get into this, I need to keep going or I'll forget what I've added."

"What're you makin'?"

"Christmas cookie dough. I'll chill it this morning and then Hayley and I will bake and decorate the cookies this afternoon. Want to help?"

"Wish I could." He'd never made Christmas cookies and doing it with Hayley and her momma would be fun. "But I promised Zane I'd check out his raptor operation this afternoon."

"No worries." Virginia put in a teaspoon of this and a teaspoon of that. "Hayley and I make Christmas cookies every year, so you'll get a chance next time."

"Yes, ma'am." His conscience gave him a little kick and he avoided looking at Hayley.

"There, that does it." She stepped back from the bowl and turned to Badger. "I'll mix it after you two leave. But I wanted to check with you about tonight's menu. We're having chili, cornbread and a side salad. Are you okay with that?"

"Sounds mighty fine to me."

"Good. Why don't you come at five? That way you and Luke will have a chance to get acquainted before we sit down to eat."

"I'll do that." He glanced at Hayley. "Ready to get some breakfast?"

"Sure am. I'll grab my coat." She left the kitchen.

Badger put on his hat and smiled at Virginia. "We'll be off then. See you tonight."

"I'm looking forward to it."

"Me, too." He paused. He didn't want her to fret if Hayley didn't come home until past noon. "Listen, do you need Hayley back at any certain time this mornin'?"

"Not really. Why?"

He lowered his voice. "It's a surprise. I've scheduled a sleigh ride."

Her eyes sparkled with excitement. "How romantic." She moved closer. "Is that it? Just a sleigh ride?"

His cheeks warmed. "Well, I—"

"You sly devil, you. I'll bet you have a certain item in your pocket."

Now his face was hot. Could she have guessed? "Um…"

"Never mind. I can be surprised, too. But what a perfect setting. Although you'd better not get down on one knee in the—"

"I'm ready to go." Hayley walked into the kitchen with her parka zipped and her purse over her shoulder.

"Then let's do it." He tipped his hat to Virginia. "See you tonight."

She gave him a conspiratorial wink. "See you then!"

Great. In trying to keep her from worrying about her daughter, he'd created a whole new problem.

14

"Badger, do you think my mom sounded a little weird when we left?" Hayley fastened her seat belt and glanced at him. "Or am I getting paranoid?"

He blew out a breath. "It's my fault. I mishandled the conversation and now she thinks I'm plannin' to propose this mornin' and offer you a ring." He backed out of the driveway and drove toward Main Street.

"How would she get that idea?"

"Well, we're only supposed to be goin' for breakfast, but I told her not to expect you back right away, that I'd planned a surprise. I didn't want her to worry."

"I knew it! I knew you were up to something. Is this about what I think it is?"

"What do you think it's about?"

"Us having sex." She quivered with anticipation.

He kept his attention on the road but his cheek dented as he grinned. "It might be about that."

"You found a solution?" She tried to breathe normally. Impossible.

"Could be." He braked the truck at the stop sign and turned to her. "But first we need to take care of something."

"You need to buy condoms."

"I bought those before I came over to your house. In fact, when your momma said *I'll bet you have a certain item in your pocket* I thought she was talkin' about that."

"Oh, Badger." She started to laugh. "No wonder your face was so red when I walked in."

"But when she mentioned gettin' down on one knee, that was my clue that she thought I had a ring and that's why our breakfast would take so long."

"Well, she'll just have to be mistaken about that."

"No, she won't." He put on the left blinker and turned onto Main Street. "I'm gettin' you a ring."

"Hey! No, you're not."

"Yes, I am. If I don't, your momma won't believe I'm serious about you. The whole plan could start fallin' apart. I remember seein' a jewelry store. Ah, there it is, and we even have a parkin' spot."

"Don't park in front of it."

"Why not? There's a perfect spot!"

"Go a few spaces down. We don't want anyone seeing us in front of the jewelry store."

"Oh. Good point." He parked in front of the hardware store and shut off the motor. "Your momma thinks I already have the ring."

"Right." She turned to him. "You don't have to buy one. Let's brainstorm."

"Let's not." The clock was ticking. He didn't want to waste time debating the ring purchase. "People don't know me here. I can duck down to the jewelry store, get a ring and come back."

"Even if you could, I can't let you do this. That's taking this charade too far."

"Hayley, if you don't show up with a ring, I guarantee your momma's opinion of me will suffer."

She met his gaze without saying anything. He was right, damn it. "Okay. Go find a ring. But I'm paying for it."

"No, you're not."

"I am, so! I'll keep the receipt and when we break up, I can just get my money back. It's the logical way to handle it. Surely you can see that."

"No, ma'am, I can't. There's no way on God's green earth that I'm lettin' you pay for the engagement ring I put on your finger."

"Badger! Be sensible!"

"I can't be sensible about this. I'm Southern."

"What's that supposed to mean?"

"No Southern gentleman would ever walk into a jewelry store to buy an engagement ring and let his lady pay. She might as well cut off his balls and hand them to him on a platter."

"I see." Her easy-going Badger had taken a stand. His display of stubborn masculinity was more of a turn-on than she would have expected. "But if you're determined to do this, I don't want a diamond."

"You don't?" He looked stunned. "Isn't that supposed to be the—"

"I've never liked them that much. I'd rather have a sapphire."

"Ah." He smiled. "One to match your eyes."

"That's not the reason. I just think they're prettier than diamonds."

"So are your eyes. I'll find a ring that matches." He opened the driver's side door.

"Wait."

"What?"

"Whoever helps you, ask them to keep this quiet. It might work, at least for a while."

"I'll do that." Leaning over, he gave her a quick kiss before exiting the truck.

A half-hour later, he was back.

"Well?"

"Found the perfect ring."

"Can I see it?"

"No. I'll give it to you later. When I propose."

"Badger! This is all make-believe. Show me the ring."

"No, ma'am." He started the truck. "When you tell your momma about the proposal, I want it to be as close to the truth as possible."

"Are you going to propose over breakfast in a restaurant?"

He sent her a smile. "No, ma'am, I am not."

Despite herself, she was intrigued. But she tried to keep the mood businesslike. "You have the receipt, I hope."

"Oh, yeah." He pulled it out of his coat pocket.

"Let me see it." She plucked it out of his hand.

"Hey, I didn't—"

"Badger Calhoun, you spent a fortune on this ring!"

"Did not."

"You did! And I—"

"Never mind, darlin'." He backed out of the parking space. "I didn't mean for you to see how much I spent, but now that you have the receipt, you'd best keep it."

"But you'll be the one who has to return it since you put it on your card."

"Just hang onto it for now, okay?"

"Okay." How easily he'd spent the money to buy a sapphire ring. Judging from what her mom and dad had found out online, his parents were very well off. Quite likely he was, too.

It didn't matter if he was or wasn't, but it gave her an idea. "We still haven't decided on an issue we can use to explain our breakup. How about money?"

"Now there's a borin' thing to fight about if I ever heard one."

"But couples do. Like for example, I could assume after going through this ring-buying experience that you throw your money around. If that's true, I would object to that behavior."

"So would I. Do you throw your money around?"

"No, but my job isn't a particularly high-paying one. I have to be careful."

"I'm careful."

"You call buying a ring on the spur of the moment careful?"

"I do. I checked out the framed certificates on the wall. That gentleman has owned that store goin' on forty-two years. He's a certified gemologist and past president of the Eagles Nest Rotary Club. He sponsors a Little League team."

"So?"

"A man like that will carry quality merchandise. Today I invested in a sapphire ring. A few months ago, I invested in Cowboy's Beechcraft and nobody's more likely to make a success of his business than he is. I'm careful with money."

"I'm glad to hear—"

"I can't claim to be so careful when I'm dealin' with people, though. Cowboy says I tend to leap into situations without thinkin' about the consequences. He could have a point."

"You may not always be careful, but you're compassionate. You came to my rescue and saved this holiday for me. Maybe you jumped in, but I'm grateful you did. I'll take good care of your investment."

"Just take good care of you, darlin'. In the end, the ring is just a pretty rock."

"It's more than that! You just said you invested in a piece of quality jewelry."

He smiled at her. "Only to show you that I don't throw money around. When I spend it, I have a good reason. But you're a million times more valuable than that ring."

She blinked. That sounded an awful lot like what an actual fiancé would say. Yet the engagement was make-believe, right? Sure, they had chemistry through the roof, but what he'd just said wasn't about sex. It was about caring. His comment wrapped her in cozy warmth from head to toe.

Distracted by their discussion, she'd lost track of where they were. A quick check out the window told her they'd left the main road and were tooling along a dirt one. "Where are we?"

"On our way to the Nestin' Place B&B."

"Say what?"

"I asked Cody about a hotel or B&B and he suggested this place. He gave me the phone number last night after dinner. I called and got us the last room she had available, the one at the top."

She couldn't make sense of it. "Badger, we can't move out of where we are and stay here. I can't leave my folks' house to..." Spend the holiday in bed with him? It was tempting.

"We're not doin' that. I figure we'll only be here an hour or so this mornin'. But maybe tomorrow mornin' we can—"

"You rented it again for tomorrow, too?"

"Darlin', I rented it through New Year's."

"I'm speechless."

"See, when Cody caught us makin' out in the tack room, that started a discussion between Cody and me. He remembered this cute little B&B that's only been open for a couple of years. Locals don't stay here. Just folks passin' through. We can pop in and out without stirrin' up gossip in town."

She stared at him. This was so out of her experience. "You rented it for more than a week?"

"Maybe that was overly optimistic. You might decide after today that you're not fond of gettin' naked with me."

"Badger, this is a very rude question but I'll ask it anyway. How much money do you have?"

"Enough."

"Enough for what?"

"The rest of my life."

"Good Lord." She flopped back against the seat. "I had no idea."

"It doesn't matter."

"No, I suppose it doesn't, except that it allows you to buy sapphires and rent a room in what is likely a pricey B&B when you'll only be using it an hour here and an hour there."

"Like I said, I'm hopin' for two hours tomorrow. But you might decide against the plan. You have veto power."

"I can't imagine vetoing anything after what's happened so far."

"I'm countin' on that. You heat up fast, Hayley. We'll make good use of that hour." He pulled up in front of a three-story blue Victorian with yellow trim.

Stately pines rose like protective sentinels behind the house. In a graded area to the side, several cars with out-of-state plates were parked. A hanging wooden sign in the snowy front yard was artistically lettered with *The Nesting Place B&B, Maureen Stanislowski, proprietor.* A spectacular evergreen wreath hung on the front door and large potted poinsettias stood guard at either side of it.

He shut off the engine. "This is it. We get a bed and we get breakfast."

"It's an inspired idea, Badger. The house is lovely." She shivered in delicious anticipation at the prospect of sharing a bedroom with him, even for an hour.

"I asked her to put the food in our room. We don't have time to fraternize at the breakfast table with the other guests."

"That's a good plan, but is she okay with this unusual arrangement?"

"I explained the situation and she was extremely understandin'. She wants us to have private time together and is very happy that she can help." He looked over at her and reached for her hand. "She told me she'd be in the back servin' breakfast, but she'll come out to meet us and give us a key."

She nodded. No man had ever swept her off her feet and she liked it. A lot.

He gazed into her eyes. "I want you, darlin'. If you'll come inside with me, you'll make me a very happy man."

Her heart thudded against her ribs. "Then let's go in."

"Thank you." After helping her out of the truck, he took her hand as they walked up to the house and climbed the steps.

She couldn't shake the image of a bride arriving at her honeymoon suite. Silly, but nothing about this was familiar.

In her experience, love affairs began late at night after a steamy date that had ended at her apartment or his. Sex had just happened. Or maybe the guy had planned for it to happen, but not to the point where he'd booked a romantic setting to seal the deal.

Badger had pulled out all the stops. Breakfast and a bed awaited them on the top floor of this stately Victorian. The fantasy would only last a few days, but for now, it was more real than she'd expected.

When Badger opened the front door, a bell tinkled. She stepped into a fairyland of twinkling lights, several miniature trees in various coordinated color schemes, and the scent of cinnamon and nutmeg in the air. Down the hallway, conversation and laughter blended with the clank of plates and silverware.

A petite woman dressed in jeans and a red Christmas sweatshirt hurried toward them from that direction. "Badger Calhoun?"

He swept off his hat. "Yes, ma'am. This is my fiancée, Hayley Bennett."

Her brow furrowed. "Bennett? Isn't Reverend Bennett the minister who's such a cutup?"

"That's my father. As Badger probably explained, I'm staying at the parsonage and Badger is out at Wild Creek Ranch. We didn't realize that we'd miss each other so much when we planned this trip, but it's been more difficult than we anticipated."

"I'm so glad you came to me, and that I had the top floor room." She handed them two keys. "The one with the blue key fob is for the front door. The green one is for your room. That will allow you to access your room at any hour."

Badger took both keys. "Thank you, ma'am. We appreciate this more than we can say."

"You're welcome. When's the happy day?"

"We're still debatin' that topic." Badger took off his jacket and helped Hayley with her parka. He put both coats over his arm. "Thank you for providin' us with a safe harbor. We'll let you get back to your guests, now." He swept his hat toward the stairs. "After you, darlin'."

15

Maybe it was the ring. Badger had never bought a woman a ring before. When he'd slipped this one in his jacket pocket, their caper had shifted from a lark to something more significant.

But they weren't engaged. The ring was an empty symbol of something that didn't exist. And yet...something had changed.

He followed her up two flights of stairs to their hideaway. Naturally the prospect of having sex up there jump-started his libido. Besides, she had a great-looking ass and her jeans fit real nice.

Except he didn't focus on that. Instead he kept looking at her bare ring finger each time she rested her left hand on the polished wooden bannister.

Once he gave her the sapphire, she might plan to return it, but he had no such plans. She could wear it, sell it or throw it off the cliff they'd ridden out to yesterday. He wasn't taking it back.

By the time he was halfway up the second flight, he had a view of the third-floor landing and the open bedroom door beyond it. Good. He wouldn't have to remember which key was which. Down in the lobby, Hayley had been standing in a shaft of sunlight that had made her hair gleam like the gold hood ornament on his father's Bentley. He'd been mesmerized by that during the instruction about keys.

Through the open bedroom door, he got a glimpse of a four poster and snowy bed linens. Then she reached the landing and blocked the view of the doorway.

Pausing, she turned back to him. He wasn't sure what to expect until she clutched the front of his shirt, stood on tiptoe and gave him an open-mouthed kiss.

There was nothing tentative about it, either. She went all in. With a groan, he wrapped her in his arms, crushing both coats but keeping a protective grip on his hat. That hot kiss of hers was having a predictable effect on his package.

He started backing them through the open door. Once they cleared it, he nudged it shut and continued the maneuver until she came up against the side of the bed. He tossed the coats aside, not caring where they landed. But he broke the kiss long enough to hang his hat on the bedpost.

She glanced at it and laughed. "I like that."

"I like this better." Recapturing her mouth, he slid his hands under her hips and lifted her until she sat on the bed with her legs dangled off the side. Perfect height for kissing.

Settling his hips between her thighs, he feasted on her mouth while he searched for the hem of her sweater. Then he paused and lifted his head. "I should've asked." He took a quick breath. "Breakfast first, or—"

"You. I want you first." Reaching down, she took hold of her sweater and whipped it over her head.

"I was hopin' you'd say that."

"Priorities." Gulping for air, she tugged on his shirt and a few snaps came undone. "I want this off, too."

"Yes, ma'am." He stepped away from the bed, unsnapped his cuffs and pulled the shirt over his head. When he looked at her, she'd taken off her bra. He let out a breath. "Oh, Hayley…"

She motioned with both hands. "Come back over here."

Crossing to the bed, he took her by the shoulders and guided her down. "I have an idea." Bracing himself on his forearms, he tucked his aching package between her thighs as he surveyed the tempting territory beneath him. "I'm goin' to start with your sweet mouth and work my way down."

"I have an idea, too." She smoothed her hands over his shoulders. "Lift up a little. Last night I barely got to touch you."

"Glad to oblige. Long as I get my turn." He straightened his arms.

Slowly she explored his chest with her soft hands. She rubbed and stroked and squeezed until his pulse rate hovered in the red zone. Usually he didn't care whether a woman loved on his pecs, but with Hayley, all bets were off.

"I like doing this." Her voice was breathy, seductive. "You have such hard muscles, such springy hair." She raked her nails lightly over his skin. "Yummy."

He shivered.

"Does that feel good?" She scratched gently, moving her hands in circles, pausing to pinch his nipples.

He swallowed. "Mm." Her breasts rose and fell rapidly as her breathing picked up. Lowering himself again, he brushed his mouth over hers. "My turn."

Beneath his kiss, her mouth curved into a smile and she let her arms fall to her sides.

Taking that as permission, he kissed his way down the curve of her throat and slowly made his way to one plump breast. She gasped as he began to lick and nibble.

He swore she tasted like whipped cream on his tongue. Her soft moans and whimpers increased the pain in his privates, but his mouth was in sensual heaven. He could do this all day if he didn't have to worry about the pressure cooker behind his fly.

He returned to her lips, urged them to open and thrust his tongue deep. She responded by grabbing his belt loops and wedging him deeper between her thighs.

Message received. Abandoning the joy of kissing her, he began working her out of her jeans and panties. Happy days and hallelujah, she elected to help him. After he'd shoved them most of the way, she kicked them off herself. Her loafers went flying and came down on the wooden floor with a loud clatter. Now that was enthusiasm.

He intended to reward that enthusiasm. He was out of his boots, jeans and boxers in no time. Grabbing his jeans, he pulled a condom out of the pocket. After he ripped it open, he threw the wrapper over his shoulder. Get that later, too.

She watched him, blue eyes bright with passion, her body quivering, her breasts still damp from his mouth. She let out a sweet little whimper. "Hurry."

"I'm hurryin' fast as I can." He rolled the condom in place. Then he scooped her up and laid her back down lengthwise on the bed. They needed plenty of room to maneuver.

Climbing onto the mattress, he moved between her thighs. "Wrap your legs around me, darlin'. I'm comin' in."

She followed his instructions, and those long legs sliding against his skin nearly destroyed his control. Jaw tight, he probed once to make sure she was ready for him. Oh, yeah.

Holding her gaze, he eased in, slow and steady. Too fast and this would be over before it began. Once he was locked in tight, he decided to hang out there and get a grip. This was so right it was scary.

She dug her fingertips into his glutes. "Badger...I want..."

"We'll get there." The strain of maintaining control made him sound like a mating bullfrog. "But you can't rush these things." He drew back and pushed forward again at the same gentle pace.

She began to pant. "Sure you can. You can rush. Please rush."

"Ever see a moonshiner's still explode?" He continued his unhurried stroke.

Her laughter sounded strangled. "Badger!"

"If I rush, then it'll be like that." He clenched his teeth against the urge to come, even though he should be able to maintain at this level. But Hayley's welcoming body was a game changer.

"That's what I want." She sucked in a breath. "Explosions. Moonshine all over the place."

"No, you don't. We'd make a lot of noise and alert the entire house."

"Speak for yourself. I won't make a lot of noise."

"Wanna bet?" He never could resist a challenge. He picked up the pace. It was rough on him because he was right on the edge, but from the way her eyes darkened, she had nearly tipped over it.

"I'll...take that bet." The faster he moved, the tighter she held on.

She would make noise. He knew it in his bones. He could say the hell with it, barrel on through and make his point, but this was their special moment. He didn't want to share it with strangers.

Instead of tearing along at a speed that would make them both crazy, he slowed down.

"Badger?"

"You're goin' to come, darlin', but when you do, I'll be there for you." He shifted the angle. There. The first spasm. The first catch in her breath.

"That's it." He kept moving as the color in her cheeks bloomed and her sapphire eyes turned navy. "Now you're close."

Her voice was a whisper. "Yes."

"Let go, Hayley. Let go."

Her breathing grew rough and she arched her back. "*Oh.* Badger, I'm—"

He covered her mouth with his, muffling her cries as her climax roared through her. He held her tight as she trembled and shook beneath him. Then he lifted his head and gazed down at her, so flushed and beautiful in the glow of release.

Her eyes were closed, but they fluttered open and she gulped in air. "Your...turn."

"Yeah." He focused on the sapphire blue in her eyes as he allowed himself to move again. Shouldn't take long. Her tight channel continued to vibrate with the aftershocks of her orgasm.

A few fast strokes and he erupted, shuddering violently in her arms. He swallowed the triumphant yell that rose to his throat. This stolen moment was theirs alone.

Eventually he roused himself and gazed down at her. He'd meant to say something funny or clever, but her beauty addled his brain. Nothing funny or clever occurred to him. Only the truth. "You were wonderful."

Her smile would melt the polar icecap. "So were you."

"Are you hungry?"

"Yes. I don't think I've ever been this hungry in my life."

"Then while I duck into the bathroom, why don't you check out what Mrs. Stanislowski left for us?"

"I'm on it."

When he returned, striding into the room naked as a jaybird, she'd put on his shirt.

"I hope you don't mind. I didn't feel like putting on my—"

"That shirt looks way better on you than it does on me." He pulled on his boxers and reached for his jeans. "But why didn't you feel like puttin' on your clothes?"

"Because this is more decadent and sexy. If all I'm wearing is your shirt, I can continue feeling that way while we eat breakfast."

"That sounds mighty promisin'. Let's eat fast."

"You might not want to. She made us each an omelet."

"She did?" He walked over to the table and lifted a silver lid covering one of the plates. "What do you know? But they have to be stone-cold by now."

"They are, but there's a small microwave on the dresser."

He glanced over there. "So there is."

"She left a note telling us it was there for warming up the omelets."

"Because she knew we'd take care of business and let them get cold. I didn't notice many details when we came in."

"Funny, neither did I." She gave him the once-over. "But we'll know this room inside out before the holidays are over."

"To hell with the room. I'd rather know you inside out."

"That can be arranged."

"So you're good with this plan?" He pulled on his jeans, zipped and buttoned them.

"I love this plan."

"Excellent." He fastened the elaborate Western belt Ryker had talked him into buying.

"That's a pretty belt buckle." Hayley walked over to take a closer look. "I didn't pay much attention to it before."

"I can understand that. You were too mesmerized by my manly physique."

She fluttered her eyelashes at him. "Yes, Badger, I was, you gorgeous hunk of burning love."

He grabbed her and pulled her close. "Keep talkin' like that and I'm liable to haul you back to bed."

"Oh, no! A fate worse than death!" She pulled his head down for a kiss.

Just like that, he was hard again. But he'd promised her breakfast. With great effort, he ended the kiss. "You said you were starving."

"Changed my mind." She combed her fingers through his hair. "The omelets are already cold. Let's eat them later."

_16_

After another amazing orgasm that nearly took off the top of her head, Hayley agreed to do the sensible thing and eat the food that Mrs. Stanislowski had made the effort to provide. Badger was fine with her wearing his shirt during the meal and she was more than fine to render him shirtless as they ate breakfast. It wasn't every day that a girl could sip coffee and stare at a chest like his.

He finished off his coffee and put down his mug. "I don't mean to rush you, but I have another surprise."

"Another one? How have you had time to arrange something else?"

"By goin' to bed late and gettin' up early."

"I believe you. Are you exhausted?"

"No, ma'am. If I could look forward to what we just had every day, I might not need to sleep at all."

"You mean the omelet."

He grinned at her. "Right, the omelet." His gaze softened. "You're the best, you know that? I can't imagine why some guy hasn't begged you to marry him."

"One did. But it wouldn't have worked."

"Why not?"

"He knew I wanted to have at least one kid, maybe two, and he was all for it."

"That sounds like a good start."

"It was. I said I wanted to keep working even if we had kids. He was fine with that, too."

Badger nodded. "Still on the same page."

"Then he promised that whenever possible, he'd help me with the kids."

"Whenever possible?"

"Uh-huh."

He let out a weary sigh. "In other words, whenever his sorry ass wasn't busy with whatever he had goin' on, he'd lend a hand."

"Yes. That's what he offered."

"He'd *help* you, but it was still your job even though they were his kids, too."

"Yes! Oh, Badger, thank you!" She left her chair and went around the table to kiss him. "You can't imagine how many guys don't get that."

"Yeah, I can." He drew her down to his lap and nestled her head against his shoulder. "I listened to soldiers for ten years. They'd brag about how much *help* they were to their wives when they went home on leave. It never dawned on them that when they weren't there, she had the entire job of raising their kids plus holdin' down a fulltime job because kids cost more than what an airman makes."

"Right." Cuddling with him was almost as much fun as sex. But he'd mentioned a surprise so she reminded him of it.

"Whoops. We need to get goin'. It's scheduled for eleven but I can probably get it moved to eleven-fifteen. It just means we won't have as much time to do it." He stood and set her gently on her feet.

"Do what?"

"Can you trust me that you'll like it and let it go at that?"

"That's a powerful lot of trust. And let me say that if it involves skydiving, you'll be horribly disappointed in my response. I'm not as plucky as I look."

"No skydivin'. But if we don't get a move on, we'll lose our window of opportunity."

"Then let's make it happen." Hayley commandeered the bathroom for a few minutes so she could dress and repair her makeup from what she carried in her purse. She hadn't brought a brush, so she finger-combed her tousled hair. Nothing to be done about the telltale flush on her cheeks.

When she came out, the covers on the bed were straightened and the dishes were stacked. Badger looked the same as he had when they're arrived at the B&B.

"How do you guys do that?"

"Do what?'

"Roll around on a mattress with a woman for an hour plus and then, when the interlude is over, you manage to pull yourself together and appear as if nothing happened."

"I have no idea what you're talkin' about." He gathered her close. "But I surely do like how you look right now."

"Like I've been playing mattress bingo?"

"Like you've been enjoyin' yourself."

"I have, Badger. Thank you for arranging this."

His brown gaze warmed. "My pleasure." He gave her a quick hug and released her. "Time to go."

When Hayley stepped out of the privacy of their room, she hoped no one would be around. She wouldn't mind staying in her cocoon of sensual bliss.

No such luck. Although no guests were in evidence, Mrs. Stanislowski sat at the reception desk working on her computer. She glanced up and took off her reading glasses. "Hello, there! Was everything all right?"

Hayley gave her a quick smile. "Yes, thank you."

"It was all perfect." Badger oozed Southern charm as he tucked an arm around Hayley's waist. "Whoever made that breakfast knows her way around a fryin' pan."

"That would be me." She gazed at him, clearly dazzled.

"Well, ma'am, it was lip-smackin' good. If you wouldn't mind puttin' breakfast up there again tomorrow, we'd be much obliged."

"Certainly. Same time?"

Badger glanced at her. "That work for you, darlin'?"

"Sure."

He tipped his hat to Mrs. Stanislowski. "Then we'll see you in the mornin'."

Once they were on their way, she turned to him. "Can you even tell me where we're going?"

"Wild Creek Ranch." He glanced at the clock on the dash. "And I'd better step on it."

"Did you send the text saying we'd be a little late?"

"I did. While you were gettin' dressed. It's no problem."

"Good." She settled back in her seat. "Does it have anything to do with Ryker?"

"No, ma'am." He chuckled. "I'm not goin' to tell you."

"At least I know we're not going up in the plane if it doesn't have anything to do with Ryker and we're headed to the ranch."

"We're not goin' up in the plane, but that would be fun sometime. There's a lot to do right now, but maybe after Christmas."

"I'd love that. I forgot to ask how long Luke's staying, but he'd love it, too."

"That's right, I'll be meetin' him tonight at dinner. Did you tell me what he does for a livin'?"

"I don't think so. He's the marketing manager for a group of upscale restaurants in Portland."

"Sounds impressive."

"It is. He makes good money, but..."

"But?"

"I don't know. He's good at it. I just never thought it fit him."

"Why not?"

"He should've been a cowboy." Then she laughed. "Like in the song. Instead he wears a tie and spends a lot of time in meetings."

"Ever ask him about it?" He turned off the main road onto the ranch road.

"Once." She gripped the armrest to steady herself over the bumps. The snow had been plowed, which left frozen ruts.

"What'd he say?"

"After putting all that money and effort into getting a business degree, he felt obligated to make use of it."

"I know how that feels."

"You do?" She hadn't meant to lead up to the subject of his college days, but this was the perfect opening. Maybe he'd tell her what she already knew. Then she wouldn't have to worry that she'd slip up and accidentally reference it.

He sighed. "Sure do. Anyway, it'll be good to meet Luke. I'm lookin' forward to it."

Or maybe he'd let the subject drop. She considered asking him directly and decided against it. He might not be in the mood to reveal elements of his past he'd rather forget.

When they got to the ranch, Badger drove over toward the barns and Hayley guessed her surprise. "A sleigh ride!"

"Yes, ma'am." He smiled at her. "Ever been on one?"

"No, I haven't!" She gazed at the green sleigh with red trim, perfect for the holiday. "I've lived in snow country all my life and always thought it would be fun. But I never made it happen. This is great! Who's the guy standing by the sleigh? I don't recognize him."

"That's Jim Underwood, Faith's dad. He's takin' us out."

"This is so cool." She was out of the truck by the time Badger walked around to get her. "You have the best ideas."

"And you have the best smile." He hooked an arm over her shoulders as they walked toward the sleigh. "Makes me want to keep comin' up with these ideas."

When they reached the sleigh, Badger introduced her to the tall, angular cowboy waiting for them.

He tipped his hat and greeted her with soft-spoken courtesy. "Call me Jim," he said. "Everyone does."

"Call me Hayley." She shook his calloused hand. "I'm so excited about this."

"Badger thought you would be."

"And who are those two fine horses you've hitched up to the sleigh?"

"This here's Bert, the taller one, and the other's Ernie, the stockier one."

"From Sesame Street?"

"Yes, ma'am. My daughter named them."

"I love those names. I watched Sesame Street." She turned to Badger. "Did you?"

"I wasn't...um, no. But I surely would like to meet these two."

Hayley glanced at Jim. "Is it okay if we say hello to Bert and Ernie?"

"Absolutely. They love attention."

As she and Badger loved on the two geldings, she was dying to ask him how come he'd never watched Sesame Street. Not now, though.

Shortly after that they were settled in the sleigh, lap robes tucked around them, and Jim climbed up to the bench seat in front. He turned around. "All set?"

"All set," Badger said.

Jim clucked to the horses, and they started off, bells jingling.

Hayley couldn't stop grinning. She turned to Badger. "I love this," she murmured. "This is about the most romantic thing I can imagine."

He wrapped an arm around her shoulders. "I told your momma about the sleigh ride and that it was a surprise."

"I'll bet she was dazzled."

"She was, although I don't think anyone could be as dazzled as you."

"Me, either. This is epic."

"And the perfect setting for this." He reached into his jacket pocket.

The ring. He was going to play it straight, too, because they had an audience. She took a shaky breath. She'd have to be equally convincing.

He must have seen the panic in her eyes, because his expression was kind and his touch gentle as he cupped her cheek. "We haven't known each other very long, darlin'."

She gulped. "No."

"But from the moment I first saw you, I knew we were meant to share somethin' special, somethin' timeless."

Her heart beat crazy fast. "I—I thought so, too."

He opened the ring box and a brilliant blue sapphire sparkled in the sun.

She stared at it, mesmerized.

With a forefinger under her chin, he tilted her face up to his and held her gaze. "Hayley Renee Bennett, will you marry me?"

She couldn't breathe.

He gave her a soft smile. "The answer I'm hopin' for is *yes*."

"Y-yes." She swallowed. *Not real, not real.*

"That makes me the luckiest man in the world." He slipped the ring on her finger. Then he leaned forward and gave her a gentle kiss before putting his lips close to her ear. "Don't want you lyin' to your momma."

Right. It wasn't real.

17

That was done. Badger accepted Jim's congratulations as the sleigh skimmed over the clean, white snow so perfectly it was almost like flying. Hayley had been subdued for a little bit, but eventually she'd started acting like her old self and seemed to be having fun.

The way she'd looked at him when he'd fake-proposed bothered him, though, like a burr he'd picked up hiking through tall grass. He'd only been trying to make sure the story she told her momma was close to the truth.

He'd expected her to find the episode amusing, but instead she'd been freaked out. His father was fond of saying *words have power*. They certainly did when Thaddeus Calhoun the Second used them in a courtroom. Evidently they also had power in a sleigh in Montana.

When the ride was over, he showered Jim with thanks and so did Hayley. They said goodbye to Bert and Ernie and climbed back in the truck.

Hayley continued to praise the sleigh ride experience as they drove away. "Loved those two horses, too," she said.

"They did a super job. I can't believe this is their first season pullin' that sleigh. Bert and Ernie were pros."

"They were. Which reminds me, why didn't you watch Sesame Street? Didn't you like it?"

"Never got a chance to find out."

"Why not?"

"My folks didn't believe TV was a good idea for kids under the age of six. Before I started school, I had tutors."

"Oh."

"Listen, Hayley, if I threw you for a loop a while ago, I'm sorry."

She didn't say anything. Didn't look at him, either.

"Ah, so I did make a mess of things. I really didn't mean to—"

"I know you didn't. You played your part exactly right. I was the one who had trouble pulling it off. How'd you know my middle name was Renee?"

"Found it online. Figured I might need to know." He peeked over at her. She was fooling with her ring, turning it around so it faced her palm, then turning it back again. He cleared his throat. "Proposin' on the sleigh ride might've been a mistake."

"Not at all." But she still wasn't looking at him. "When I had a chance to think about it, I figured out that you were only trying to make sure I had a scenario in my head for when I told the story to my mother."

"That was the plan but maybe it was a bad plan."

"It's just that things are a little confusing right now. I have this ring, which feels weird, and you've proposed, although you didn't mean it. But on the other hand, we like each other and we've had great sex."

"Is that what's throwin' a monkey wrench into it? The sex?"

"No! That's the one thing that feels real."

"So you want to keep doin' that?"

Finally she looked over at him and smiled. "Yes, please."

He let out a breath. "I'm mighty glad. But I would give it up if it's makin' things more difficult for you."

"Badger, you're not making anything more difficult for me. You stepped in to make things easier and they are. By now my mother would have paraded at least two, maybe three men in front of me with more to come. This is the best Christmas I've had in years."

"Me, too." Best Christmas ever, but he wasn't going to say that.

"We need to decide how we'll do the ring reveal, though."

"Okay."

"You'll have to come in, but you don't have to stay long."

"Which I can't. I have that thing with—"

"Zane's raptor center. I know. Just come in the house with me. I'll find Mom wherever she is, show her the ring, and she'll come screeching out into the living room to hug you. Then you can leave."

"Any chance your dad will be there?"

"Oh, yeah. He might be. He had an appointment this morning but it's lunchtime. They'll likely both be in the kitchen eating. She'll still come barreling out to hug you. Dad will be more reserved."

"Because he's worried we're rushin' things."

She reached over and squeezed his thigh. "And you're taking his feelings into account. And my mom's. That's admirable."

"Their feelings matter to me. I didn't know they would, but they do. They're good people. Your momma's way too intent on marryin' you off, but she means well."

"She does."

"That's why I want us to part amicably. I'm hopin' they won't be too upset if we can tell them we're still friends."

"*Amicably.*" She laughed. "That sounds like lawyer talk."

"I've been around it some." He pulled into the driveway of the parsonage. "Ready to do this thing?"

"Aye, aye, cap'n!" She managed a salute, but it wasn't very crisp.

He smiled and shook his head. "You need to work on that salute, soldier."

"Did you really have people salute you when you were in the Air Force?"

"Is that so hard to believe?"

"No, but it sure is sexy."

He laughed. "Whatever works. Now stay put. If anybody's lookin' out the window, I want them to see me openin' your door for you."

"Nobody's looking out the window."

"Maybe not, but after that first time, I'm paranoid about bein' watched." He rounded the front of the truck and helped her down. Her ring flashed in the sunlight. "That sapphire sure is pretty."

"It should be considering what you paid for it. I can't believe I'm wearing something worth that much money. And it doesn't do anything except sit there on my finger."

"Some things aren't supposed to be practical. They're just supposed to be beautiful."

"This ring qualifies." She spread her fingers and gazed at the deep blue stone. "There's not a single practical thing about it."

"That's not true." He caught her hand and turned it this way and that so the stone reflected the light. "It's goin' to convince your folks that I mean business."

For some reason that gave her the giggles.

"What? What did I say?"

"You sound like a gunslinger at high noon." She attempted a gruff delivery except she kept cracking up. "See this here ring?" She held up her hand and wiggled her finger. "It says I mean *business*. Don't mess with me, y'all."

"Hey, I like that approach. Would it work?"

"Dad would love it and Mom would think you'd ruined a special moment by acting goofy."

"Then we won't make jokes. I want your momma to be happy. Let's go." He followed her inside and as she'd predicted, the murmur of voices and the clink of dishes suggested her parents were at the kitchen table eating lunch.

Her dad's voice was more distinct. "I wish she'd spent more time with him, that's all. A few weekends isn't enough."

Whoops. He glanced at Hayley.

She shrugged, gave his arm a pat and walked into the kitchen.

Moments later, her mother started screeching like a teenager at a rock concert. She ran into the living room, arms extended, and gave him the hug to end all hugs. She was stronger than she looked and she nearly squeezed the breath out of him. Knocked off his hat, too.

Eventually she let go and stood back, panting. "That is the most beautiful engagement ring I have *ever* seen. Wherever did you find it?"

"That's my little secret." He retrieved his hat from the floor and dusted it off.

She pressed her hand to her chest and took several deep breaths. "Excuse me. I'm hyperventilating. I've imagined this moment for so long."

Oh, God, now he was feeling guilty. He focused on Hayley's dream of a Christmas without prospective boyfriends being shoved at her. This woman had ruined several holiday seasons for her daughter. No reason to feel guilty.

Next Warren came through the kitchen door. He was smiling, but he didn't look completely at ease. Stepping forward, he shook

Badger's hand. "That's a beautiful ring. Nice choice."

"Thank you, sir."

"I asked Hayley if you two had set a date. I was relieved to hear you haven't."

"Warren!" Virginia gave him a nudge. "Is that any way to talk to your daughter's fiancé?"

"I think it is." He held Badger's gaze. "Marriage requires a solid commitment and a plan for the future. I like you, but you seem a little adrift."

He fell back on his standard response. "I haven't been stateside very long, sir. Takes a while to get acclimated."

"I appreciate that. But my daughter just accepted your proposal. I'd feel a whole lot better if I knew you had some plans, son."

So would he. "Sir, you have my promise that before we set a date, I'll have decided what I want to do with my life. You're right to be concerned. No father worth his salt would want his daughter to marry a drifter."

Warren nodded. "Eloquently put. Hayley obviously adores you and there's nothing wrong with starting from scratch and building from there."

"That's my thought, too. Especially if you build it together."

He studied Badger. "You have promise. I'm eager to find out what that leads to."

"Speaking of promises," Hayley said, "Badger has to go. He has an appointment to tour Zane's raptor refuge."

Her father beamed. "Now there's a noble cause if I ever saw one. Zane and his brothers put together a little fundraiser at the Guzzling Grizzly last month. Virginia and I had a blast."

"It was fun." Virginia wiggled her hips. "The Whine and Cheese Club taught us some new line dances." She looked over at Badger. "Before you run off, are you hungry? I could fix you a sandwich to go."

"Thanks, but Hayley and I had a big breakfast."

"Then we won't keep you any longer. You'll be back here at five, anyway."

"Yes, ma'am. I'll see y'all then." He started out the door. Then he paused and turned around. A guy who'd just had his proposal accepted would kiss his fiancée goodbye.

Hayley covered his lapse beautifully. "It's okay, Badger." She walked over and wound her arms around his neck. "You can kiss me goodbye. Mom and Dad can handle it."

"Oh, we certainly *can*," Virginia said.

"Yes, we can," Warren said, "but let's allow them some privacy and go finish our lunch."

"Of course, of course. I'm just so happy that Hayley's—"

"I know, sweetheart." He put his arm around her shoulders and propelled her back toward the kitchen. "I know."

Badger drew Hayley closer. "Thanks for the save. This bein' engaged takes some gettin' used to."

"For me, too." She lowered her voice. "Don't mind Dad. He doesn't need to know your plans and he especially doesn't need to find out you're financially independent."

"I like that he doesn't know that. He treats me like a regular guy. I didn't tell any of my buddies in the Air Force, either. Then I had to confess it to Ryker before he'd take the money for my half of the plane."

"And I flat out asked you."

"I can see why. The ring and the B&B reservation caught your attention."

"Luckily my dad knows nothing about the price of jewelry. My mom's slightly more knowledgeable, but I doubt she'd ever guess how expensive this was. She might think it was cheaper because it's not a diamond."

"That would be great. I hope everybody thinks that."

"My point is, you don't have to come up with a set of goals to please my father."

"What if I come up with a set of goals to please myself?"

"That's up to you." She hesitated. "Do you want to?"

"Yeah. Yeah, I do. Ryker's already pointed out that after being told what to do for ten years, it's now up to me to organize my days. Which means I need a job, one that makes me excited to get up in the mornin'."

"Then I hope you find one that gets your juices flowing." She rose to her tiptoes and kissed him gently on the mouth before stepping back. "Now skedaddle or you'll be late."

"Speaking of juices..." He pulled her in tight. "I need more than a little taste to get me through the next few hours." He settled his mouth over hers and took the kiss deep, so deep that he finally had to back away or risk leaving the parsonage with a full-blown erection.

She gasped for air. "Badger, that was—"

"More than you bargained for." He sounded like a long-distance runner at the finish line. "I know." Breathing hard, he backed toward the door. "Got carried away."

Her eyes sparkled like the sapphire on her finger. "I like that in a person."

Cramming his hat on his head, he touched two fingers to the brim and left. Sometime later he pulled up in front of the Raptors Rise visitor center and had no idea how he got there. Hayley had been front and center the entire drive.

Get it together, Calhoun. Scrubbing a hand over his face, he climbed out of the truck and entered a room filled with windows and light. Life-sized black cutouts of raptors in flight decorated the ceiling, each with a label identifying the bird. An easel stood nearby with informational pamphlets tucked in various pockets of the board propped on it.

No one sat at the sleek wooden receptionist's desk. Badger glanced at his phone and by some miracle he was right on time. Must be his military training kicking in.

Then Zane came down a hallway to the right. Badger had expected him to look different when he was over here, maybe wear a dress shirt and pants, but no, he still looked like a cowboy complete with a hat.

"Hey, Badger!" He extended his hand and clapped him on the shoulder. "Sorry I wasn't here to meet you. My volunteer's out having lunch. She should be back in a few minutes. Can I get you anything? Water? Coffee?"

"Thanks, I'm good."

"Then let's get on with the tour. There's one place I want to show you first thing. I think you'll like it." He gestured down the hallway he'd just come out of. "It's this way."

"I expect I'll like all of it."

Zane grinned. "Yeah, we get that a lot. People love these birds. I'm guessing you and Ryker have a special understanding after spending so much time in the air like they do."

"That's the truth. I was sittin' on the banks of the Chattahoochee one day watchin' a hawk and that's when I decided to join the Air Force."

"Do you miss flying?"

"I do."

"Ryker sure would like to have you join him."

"I know. I'm thinkin' about it." And every damned time he did, his parents' voices yammered at him about wasting his education and his opportunities. Now that he was back, he had one more chance to redeem himself. If he chose Montana and Badger Air, they'd never forgive him.

"Well, here we are." Zane paused outside a closed door. "Welcome to the Badger Calhoun Raptor Nursery."

"The what?"

Zane pointed to the plaque next to the door. "This is what I did with your donation, so it seemed right to put your name on it."

Badger stared at his name engraved on the brass plaque. "I'll be damned. I didn't expect that you'd—"

"I know, but that was a hell of a lot of money. And I thought you'd get a kick out of having your name on the nursery. I asked Ryker if I should use Thaddeus instead, and he said that would be a big mistake."

"Yeah, it would have been." He turned to Zane. "I'm honored. Thank you."

"Are you kidding? I'm the one who's grateful. We needed a special room to house the nestlings. When I first started, we didn't get many babies, but that's changing now that the word's out."

"Are there any in there?"

Zane shook his head. "Wrong time of year. If you show up next spring, you can see it in operation." He opened the door. "Right now it's just empty cages and boxes of supplies. But go on in and look around, anyway."

"I'd like that." He walked the perimeter of the room checking out the cages and the examining table. He'd helped make this happen. That was a good feeling. A very good feeling.

He glanced at Zane leaning in the doorway. "I'll be back in the spring."

_18_

Luke was due any minute, and Hayley had trouble concentrating on the cookie decorating. She was eager to see him and she dreaded seeing him. If Badger hadn't bought her a ring, she would have tried to downplay his importance in her life. That option was gone.

She would have liked her dad to be here when Luke arrived, but he'd left to meet with a parishioner. His calming presence would have muted her mom's enthusiastic raving about the prospective son-in-law.

Maybe it would help if she ran out to meet her brother and got the first word in. When a car pulled into the driveway, she leaped up. "I'll bet that's Luke!"

"I'm sure you're right!" Her mom jumped up, too. "Let's go meet him."

So much for that strategy. "Can't wait to see him!" She ran out the door without her coat, which gave her a few seconds lead.

"Hayley! Your jacket!"

Luke climbed out of the car and she ran straight into his arms. "I'm engaged."

"You're *what*?" He held her away from him and his brown eyes narrowed. "Did you say *engaged*?"

"Yes, and I—"

"She's engaged!" Her mom raced down the walkway, her jacket unzipped. "Hayley, show him the ring!"

She held up her left hand. "It's not a diamond."

"I see that. It's one hell of a sapphire, though." He lifted his gaze to hers. "Is your guy that well-off? I could be wrong, but I'm betting that's a pricey ring."

"I thought it looked expensive, too," her mom said. "Which shows how much he loves her. Come here, Luke. Give your mom a hug. I've missed you."

Hayley stood aside.

"Missed you, too, Mom." Luke embraced her warmly.

She stepped back and smiled at him. "Isn't it fabulous that your sister's engaged?"

"Sure is a surprise." He glanced over at Hayley. "I didn't even know you were getting serious about someone."

She cringed at the ribbon of hurt running through his words. "It...happened fast."

"Must have." His expression softened. "Aw, never mind, sis. You were just busy being in love. Must be a great guy. Where are you hiding him?"

Her throat tightened. Luke was such a sweetie. So ready to forgive and forget. "He's not staying here, but—"

"He'll be here for dinner," her mom said.

"I'm confused. Why isn't this guy staying here? No, wait. Before you answer that, tell me his name. I can't keep calling him *this guy* if he's going to become a member of the family."

Hayley hugged herself to ward off the cold. "His n-name is B-badger."

"Ba-badger?" Then he took a closer look at her. "Has love made you stupid? What are you thinking, coming out with no coat?"

"I told her to put on her coat."

Luke closed the car door and pocketed the keys. "Yeah, Mom, but we know Hayley has a mind of her own. Right, sis?" He wrapped a protective arm around her and started for the porch.

"R-right."

"I'll make hot chocolate," her mom said as they headed into the house.

"Sounds great, Mom. And I'd offer to build a fire in the fireplace, except, oh, look, there's no fireplace. How does a parsonage in Montana not have a fireplace?"

"Your father asked the same thing when we moved here. They said the minister they built it for didn't want one."

"Well, that's just wrong." Luke grabbed an afghan off the back of the couch and gave it to Hayley. "Wrap up in this."

"Thanks." She wound herself in the soft afghan and sat on the couch. Luke joined her there, turning to face her. "Okay, let's try again. What's your fiancé's name?"

"Badger."

"No, I mean his first name."

"That's it. Badger Calhoun."

"Is he Native American?"

"He's Southern!" came the answer from the kitchen. "That's his nickname. His real name is Thaddeus."

"Thanks, Mom!" Luke grinned at Hayley. "Guess if somebody named me Thaddeus I'd pick something else, too. So why isn't he staying here? Are Mom and Dad still that strict about—"

"No, we're not!" their mom called out. "Hayley, tell him it's not our fault that he's staying somewhere else."

Luke rolled his eyes. "Do you want to forget about the hot chocolate so you can be a part of this conversation?"

"No, I want to make it for you kids. You always loved it."

"Thanks, Mom." Luke exchanged a smile with Hayley and leaned closer. "Ain't it great to be ten years old again?"

She laughed. "Sure is."

"Okay, so we've established that Badger is Southern and hates his given name. Where is he, now?"

"Out at Wild Creek Ranch. He was in the Air Force with Ryker McGavin and he's partly here to visit him."

"Don't know anything about the ranch, never heard of Ryker McGavin. That's what I get for only coming for Christmas." He gazed at her. "Forgive me, but this seems like a very complicated courtship. How did you two get to know each other?"

She gave him the story she and Badger had cooked up, but she could tell from the skeptical gleam in his eyes he wasn't buying it.

He leaned toward her again and kept his voice down. "Are you pregnant?"

"No!" Then she clapped her hand over her mouth. Talk about over-reacting.

"I had to ask, because this quick engagement has a one-night-stand-gone-wrong vibe."

"I'm not pregnant." She was tempted to explain the plan. But right then, her mom came in carrying a tray loaded with whipped-cream-topped mugs of hot chocolate and a plate of freshly baked Christmas cookies.

"Now this is what Christmas is all about." Luke stood and helped distribute the goodies.

With her mom in attendance, Hayley had no choice but to keep the fantasy going. By the time five o'clock rolled around, Luke knew what Hayley could reveal about Badger, which wasn't much. She'd thrown out a comment about lawyer talk today in hopes he'd confirm that his dad was a lawyer. He hadn't. She'd leave it up to her mom to tell what she'd learned on the Internet.

Interestingly, her mom chose not to do that, even though she had time before Badger was due at the house. Her dad came home and gave his typical measured evaluation of Badger but he didn't mention the info from the Internet, either.

Hayley admired their restraint. Maybe they were becoming protective of him now that he'd come up with a ring. As he'd said, the ring announced that he meant business, especially because there was nothing puny about it. Luke's quick evaluation of the sapphire indicated he'd picked up some expertise on gemstones, maybe from rubbing elbows with wealthy restaurant owners.

Badger arrived on the dot of five with a bottle of red wine and a holiday floral arrangement. Her heart squeezed. He'd agreed to this charade and he was going all in.

Luke was cordial, because Luke was always cordial. But he was clearly sizing up this man who'd evidently won his sister's hand. In a subtle way, he seemed to be daring Badger to prove himself worthy.

"So, Badger," Luke said halfway through the meal. "Since you're from Atlanta, what do you think about the zombie apocalypse?"

Her dad nearly killed himself laughing. "I asked him the same thing!"

"Yeah, well, the apple doesn't fall far from the tree and all that." Luke gazed across the table at Badger. "My dad beat me to it, so I guess you don't have to answer."

"I'm happy to answer." Badger smiled at him. "I've spent ten years fightin' all manner of insurgents. If the zombie apocalypse happens, I'm as prepared as anyone and maybe better'n most."

Her mother clapped wildly. "Bravo, Badger!"

Luke raised his glass in Badger's direction. "Then I want you on my side." He held Badger's gaze and something passed between them.

Hayley couldn't say for sure, but it might be mutual respect. And surprise, surprise, she wanted that, even if Badger was her fake fiancé. But he'd also become her friend, and she'd like for her trusty friend and her beloved brother to get along, at least for the duration of the holidays.

* * *

Badger had squared off against clever guys like Luke before, but never in this context. He'd met them in his pre-law classes and in flight training. His technique was to disarm them with his Southern accent. Some people believed a Southern accent automatically branded a person a hillbilly.

Luke wasn't one of those people. But then Luke had him linked up with Hayley and wouldn't believe his sister would choose someone who couldn't hold his own. They moved from the topic of zombies to fighter jets, which put Badger squarely in his wheelhouse. But Luke had been crazy about jets as a kid and had kept up with the subject as an adult.

That conversation resulted in Badger inviting Luke to go for a ride in the Beechcraft when he took Hayley up. He was rewarded by Hayley's happy smile. Turned out he and her brother had more in common than he would have guessed. Gradually, the element of competition disappeared and they relaxed into a conversation between two guys interested in many of the same things.

Making friends with Luke wasn't logical. When the relationship ended after the holidays, Badger might be able to hold onto his friendship with Virginia and Warren. But Luke, not so much. The guy was fiercely loyal to his sister. If the breakup caused her any distress, Luke would blame him, not her.

Toward the end of the meal, Luke asked one of the questions Badger had been dreading. "Have you two decided where you want to live?"

Badger had no interest in picking up that hot potato so he turned to Hayley. "You want to take that one, darlin'?"

"Sure." She smiled at her brother. "We haven't worked that out yet. So much depends on what Badger decides to do. But that boat has sailed for me. My job's in Denver. I don't plan to give it up."

Badger responded to his cue. "I would never ask you to." He turned to Luke. "I'm the loose cannon in this operation and I freely admit it. Your dad has already said he'd prefer to have his future son-in-law gainfully employed."

Luke gave him a speculative glance. "Unless it doesn't matter."

"Meaning?"

"You invested in your Air Force buddy's plane. You bought my sister what looks like a very high-priced engagement ring. I don't think you did that by saving up your military pay."

Virginia started fluttering like a distressed momma bird. "Luke, that's none of our business."

Luke glanced at his father. "Do you think it's our business, Dad?"

Warren nodded. "Now that you mention it, yes, I do." He looked across the table at Badger. "Where's all this money coming from, son? I understand that's normally a rude question to ask, but under the circumstances, I feel it's justified."

Badger took a deep breath. They were right. "Before I was born, my parents established a trust fund in my name. I got control of it when I turned twenty-five. I educated myself about investments and I've been fortunate."

Silence descended. Under the table, Hayley nudged her knee against his. "Badger didn't want you to know about this, Dad. He told me earlier today he liked that you were treating him like a regular guy."

She was coming to his aid, putting his actions in a favorable light. Behaving like a true friend. In that moment, he lost a piece of his heart.

Warren gazed at Badger. "I would have treated you the same even if I'd known. I don't care if you have several million sitting in that trust fund, and from what you've said you just might. But you still need a plan, a goal, something you're striving for."

"Yes, sir. I couldn't agree more."

"But make sure you think long and hard about what you want that to be," Luke said. "I thought I had the perfect plan. I didn't."

"What are you talking about?" If Virginia had been agitated before, that was nothing compared to her anxiety, now. "What do you mean? You have a great job with a great future."

"I've been telling myself the same thing for years. I've finally admitted it's not for me."

"Oh, Luke."

"I'm sorry, Mom. But I'll be fine. It just occurs to me that Badger has the financial security to take his time and make the right choice. That's a luxury."

Badger nodded. "I'm aware of that."

"Choose wisely."

"That's good advice." Now if only he knew what the wise choice was.

The rest of the evening's conversation centered on Luke's decision to leave his job. Grateful to be out of the spotlight, Badger was in a mellow mood when he said his goodbyes.

Hayley put on her coat and walked as far as the porch steps with him. "I think it's colder tonight."

"Could be." He drew her into his arms. "But it's mighty warm on this porch."

"That it is." She nestled against him. "You handled that well."

"Thanks. Are we still on for breakfast in the mornin'?"

"Wouldn't miss it for the world." And she pulled his head down for a kiss that left no doubt.

He didn't know how this crazy plan of theirs would turn out in the end, but he had a breakfast date with Hayley, and that would make him very eager to get up in the morning.

_19_

Hayley loved her brother for many reasons, but currently she adored him for taking the focus off her and Badger. When she returned to the living room, her folks were in a deep discussion with Luke about his future. She stayed to participate until she couldn't keep her eyes open any longer. Then she made her excuses and went to bed.

Luke slept in the next morning. When she announced to her mom and dad that Badger was taking her to breakfast, they both smiled and told her to have fun. Badger poked his head into the kitchen to say a quick hello. They responded but didn't start up a conversation.

"Your folks seem distracted." Badger backed the truck out of the drive.

"They're worried about Luke. They thought he was all set, career wise, and now he's admitted that he's unhappy and wants to shift gears."

"To what?"

"I went to bed before the three of them finished talking last night, so I don't know the whole story, but I got the impression he doesn't know for sure. He's just sick of a job where he's expected to wear a tie every day and spend most of his time indoors. In restaurants, specifically."

"You told me that job didn't fit him."

"I don't think it does, so this doesn't come as a shock to me, but my parents seem shook up. Well, Mom is. Dad's trying to get her to see the positive side."

"I see a huge positive side. He's figured out he hates his job and he doesn't have a family to worry about. Better to make a change now."

"I think so, too. But my mom assumed his future was mapped out and she didn't have to worry about that part of his life. She doesn't like that his plans are up in the air."

"That's not surprisin'. It must be tough to be a parent. You want the best for your kid. Then they reach the age where they can go off and do whatever they want, whether you think it's a good idea or not."

She gazed at him. "Like you did?"

"I guess you could say that."

Maybe now he'd open up about his parents and their expectations. She waited. Nothing. Clearly he didn't want to talk about it.

And why should he, especially if it was a painful subject? If they'd been engaged for real, then sure. Confiding in her would be important. But they were only playing at being a committed couple.

He put on the truck's turn signal and headed down the road to the B&B. "Anyway, I hope your brother finds something that makes him happy. I like him. Seems like a great guy."

"He is. I could tell he likes you, too."

Badger chuckled. "Smoked me out, didn't he? Your folks didn't put two and two together but he did."

"He's a business consultant. He thinks in financial terms and he hangs out with people who have money. When he saw my ring, he knew it was expensive."

"It's really not *that* expensive." He pulled into the parking area beside the B&B.

"Compared to what? The Hope diamond?"

"Compared to several in my mother's jewelry box." He glanced at her. "I don't want it back. I want you to keep it."

"That's crazy."

"No, it's not." He reached for her left hand and rubbed his thumb over the surface of the stone. "I'm askin' for my sake, really."

"That makes no sense."

"To me it does." He held her gaze. "When we break up, I'm hopin' that your family won't think too poorly of me. It'll help my cause if you tell them I insisted on makin' this my partin' gift to you. Now they know I can afford it."

"Badger, I can't take this ring. It's no use trying to talk me into it."

"You're right. Talkin' is a terrible way to convince you." Heat flickered in his eyes. "Let's go upstairs."

Her breath caught. "You won't convince me that way, either."

"Maybe not, but I'll sure have fun tryin'."

How did he do that? One minute she was having a relatively calm discussion in the truck and the next she was hurrying toward the B&B, her hand held tightly in his, her pulse racing and her panties already damp.

Thank goodness Mrs. Stanislowski was nowhere to be seen as they barreled through the lobby and up the stairs. Talk about undignified. But his urgency fueled hers.

The minute he flung the door closed, he started ripping off his clothes and she yanked off hers. They were both panting by the time he shoved back the covers, grabbed her around the waist and hauled her into bed with him.

"I want you so bad, darlin'." He covered her face with hot kisses. "But first..." He gulped for air. "First I want..." He expanded his territory, nipping and nibbling her breasts until she writhed against the sheet.

Moving lower, he rubbed his open mouth over her stomach as she thrashed beneath him. At last he pinned her to the bed, one large hand gripping each of her thighs as he bestowed the most intimate kiss of all.

And she was lost, surrendering utterly to the pulse-pounding heat and the spiraling need that wrenched moans from her lips. Ah, yes. *Yes.* She climaxed in seconds, her body arching as she gasped out his name.

His weight shifted, foil crinkled and he was there, plunging into her still quivering channel, his gasps blending with hers. Faster and faster he pumped as the shock waves of her first orgasm subsided and the coil of desire tightened again.

She clutched his hips, urging him on. Sparks of pleasure flared with each vigorous thrust. And, oh, happy days, she was coming again, diving into the swirling waters of release.

He followed her, his deep groan of satisfaction rumbling in his chest, his body shuddering against hers. He stayed locked in tight as he gazed down at her, his breathing ragged.

"That was amazin'!" A slow smile of triumph spread across his handsome face.

She smiled back. "Yep."

"The last time I had that much fun I was doin' some fancy flyin' in an F-15."

"You had sex in a fighter jet?"

"No, ma'am. You could get killed tryin' that. I just meant this gave me a rush like doin' a max climb in an Eagle. That baby has thrust."

She began to giggle. "So do you, flyboy."

"Appreciate the compliment. Did I convince you to keep the ring?"

"No."

"Damn. Guess we'll have to do this again once I'm recovered." He eased away from her and left the bed.

"It's a lost cause, Badger!" she called after him.

"No such thing!" he shouted back.

Repeating yesterday's routine, she climbed out of bed and retrieved his shirt off the floor. It was a wonder he hadn't torn it in his haste. Same with her.

Putting on the shirt, she wandered over to the small table where Mrs. Stanislowski had left their breakfast, along with a single hothouse rose.

No way had their landlady grown it in the backyard.

But the sentiment was sweet. Everything about this adorable B&B was geared toward romantic couples. Couples in love. She touched the velvet petals of the rose.

Badger was getting to her. It wasn't just the sex, which was incredible. Being with him was easy and natural. Fun. More fun than she'd had in years.

But they'd started this caper to fool her mother and from all indications, he hadn't moved beyond that concept. If he had, he'd be telling her about his family. He might discuss what job options he'd considered besides Ryker's offer.

He hadn't done that. Quite the opposite. He'd clammed up whenever he'd had the perfect opening to confide in her. This morning he'd used the phrase *when we break up* as he'd announced he wanted her to keep the ring.

Coming up behind her, he drew her back against his naked body. "If you want to eat breakfast now you'd better say so, because seein' you in my shirt has given me other ideas."

She wiggled against the hard length pressed against her backside. "Can't imagine what those are."

"Are you hungry? Because I'm good at delayed gratification."

She turned in his arms and slid her palms up his bare chest. "I'm not. But let's take it slow and easy this time."

"Sounds like makin' love Southern style."

"Does it? Maybe you need to show me what that's like."

"It would be my privilege, darlin'. But first we need to get rid of this." Grasping the front of the shirt, he wrenched it apart. Snaps gave way. "There we go." He slid the shirt over her shoulders and nuzzled her throat in the process.

As he pulled the shirt past her wrists, he leaned down and tasted her breasts in a leisurely, almost lazy caress. The shirt dropped to the floor.

Then he scooped her up in his arms. "This would be the Rhett Butler move."

"Where he carries her up the staircase?"

"Right."

"But they both wore clothes and you're carrying me across level ground a maximum of ten feet."

"Inconsequential details. It's what happens after that I'm thinkin' of."

"In the movie, we don't see what happens after that."

"Exactly. We only know that the next mornin' Scarlett is very happy. That gives me latitude." He carried her to the bed and laid her gently down.

"Are you going to make me very happy?"

"Yes, ma'am." He picked up his jeans, pulled a condom from his pocket and proceeded to put it on.

"Good start."

"Thank you kindly." He climbed into bed with her. "My guess is that ol' Rhett stuck with the tried and true, so we're not goin' to do any fancy stuff."

"Okay."

Moving between her thighs, he braced his hands on either side of her head. "Let's see how makin' love Southern style works for us."

"I'm game."

"First off, I'll slide my cock in slow and easy. No sudden moves." He gazed into her eyes as he gradually entered her.

Her breathing grew shallow. It was the sexiest beginning to sex she'd ever experienced.

His eyes grew heavy-lidded as he seated himself firmly inside her. "How's that?"

"Not bad." Because he'd come in slowly, she was more aware of his length and girth. It was a snug fit. An exceedingly erotic fit, especially when he just stayed there, not moving.

Then his cock twitched.

"*Oh.*" The sensation traveled to every nerve ending in her body.

"Enjoy that?"

"Uh-huh."

"Your turn."

"My turn?"

"Squeeze."

The intimacy of it turned her blood to rivers of heat. She contracted her core muscles.

His jaw tightened.

Ha! She'd affected him the same way he'd affected her. "Like that?"

"Yes."

"Want me to do it again?"

"No." He swallowed. "I'm going to start moving at a very gentlemanly pace. Enjoy."

Rocking his hips slowly, he caressed the walls of her channel with controlled, light friction.

It was like nothing she'd ever experienced. In theory, his subtle movements should be too tame to excite her. In practice, he was driving her nuts.

And even more arousing, he was watching her as she gradually unraveled. His lazy smile added to the seductive rhythm he'd created.

"Not much to it, is there?" He maintained the pace that was dismantling her poise one unhurried stroke at a time.

"Not...much."

"Laid-back sex. I could do it all day."

"I don't believe you."

"You think I'll run out of steam?"

"No." She took a steadying breath. "I think you'll come pretty soon. Just like I will."

"Nah."

She rested her hand on his chest. "Your heart is pounding as hard as mine. You may look relaxed, but I know different. You're ready to explode."

"Am not."

"Are so."

"Am...not." He clenched his jaw.

"I'll bet you will if I do this." She tightened her core muscles.

He gasped.

"Told you." But that slight action on her part was all it took to send her over the edge. With a quick cry of surprise, she erupted, trembling beneath him as the waves of her orgasm surged through her.

He drew in a sharp breath. "You win." Abandoning his leisurely pace, he came in hard and fast. Then he delved deep, pulsing within her as he gulped for air.

Wrapping her arms around him, she urged him closer. "Come here. Cuddle with me."

He settled down with a sigh and nestled his cheek against her shoulder. He took a shaky breath. "You blow me away."

"Same here, Badger." She stroked his hair. "Same here.

_20_

Nobody was at Hayley's house when Badger took her home. Her mom had left a note that they'd gone to pick up pastries at the bakery and would be back by lunchtime. In the note, she reminded Hayley that they'd be getting the tree and decorating it that afternoon.

Badger was just as glad not to have to interact with them right now. Making love to Hayley this morning had rocked his world and he didn't know what to do about that. His life was up in the air, just like her brother's. No man with a conscience would ask a woman to sign on when his future was a jumbled mess in his mind.

But as they stood in the kitchen after she'd found the note, he pulled her into his arms because he couldn't be within five feet of her and not have the urge to do that. She didn't resist, either. Chances were good she liked it.

He tucked her head under his chin. "Thanks for havin' breakfast with me."

She chuckled. "If we're not careful, _we're going for breakfast_ will become code for having sex."

"It already is as far as I'm concerned."

"Want to stay and help with our tree?"

"I would, but this afternoon's tree-cuttin' day at Wild Creek Ranch. After that, Ryker, Cody and I scheduled one more practice for our jugglin' act."

"I can't believe the talent show is tonight already."

"I can't, either." He rubbed the small of her back. "Seems like forever since we talked to Ryker about it in the airport."

"And the vacation will be over before we know it."

"Let's not think about that."

"Okay." She lifted her head and gazed up at him. "Do you regret anything?"

"No, ma'am."

"Are you sure? It's turned into a more complicated deal than I'd anticipated."

"It has, but *havin' breakfast* with you two mornings in a row was a bonus I hadn't counted on. That makes up for any complications."

"Think we can do it again tomorrow?"

He threaded his fingers through her silky hair. "I've been considerin' that. Do you care if your family figures out what we're up to?"

She sighed. "I shouldn't care, but I'd feel kind of awkward if they know we're enjoying more than breakfast."

"So would I. And three prolonged breakfasts in a row starts lookin' suspicious. We could try it again after Christmas, but not in the mornin'."

"You're right, damn it."

"How about this? Tomorrow night after the candlelight service, we could say we're takin' a drive to see the Christmas lights around town."

"That's brilliant." Her eyes sparkled sapphire-bright. "We've never done it at night."

He grinned. "I hate disappointin' you, but my moves don't change after the sun goes down. Maybe yours do, though."

"Not really. I—"

"Maybe you're a shapeshifter." He leaned down and nuzzled the side of her neck. "Or a vampire." He nipped gently and then kissed her there.

"I'm just a flesh and blood woman." She wrapped her arms around his neck. "One who's going to heat up unless you stop doing that."

"I love that about you." He cupped her ass and squeezed. "But I'm leavin' before we get caught goin' at it on your folks' sofa." Placing a quick kiss on her mouth, he backed away. "See you at the talent show. Save me a seat."

"I will. Thanks for breakfast."

"You're welcome, darlin'." He headed out the door before he changed his mind and kissed her again.

When he parked in front of the ranch house, a giant sled sat down by the barn. A chain saw and an ax were lying on it.

Ryker, April and Kendra were in the living room rearranging furniture when Badger walked in.

"Hi, Badger," Kendra called out. "We're making room for the tree."

He looked at the space over by the front window that was now vacant. "You must be plannin' on a big tree."

"Always," Kendra said. "You wouldn't believe how many ornaments I have from the years when the boys used to make them in school."

Ryker gazed at her with fondness. "You know you don't have to keep every blessed one, Mom."

"Of course I do. This is my happiness tree. Every ornament reminds me of Christmases when you'd bring home that special thing you made for our tree. At some point, I'll let each of you have your pick, but not yet."

"That'll be fun." April placed a lamp back on an end table and her jingle bell earrings tinkled. "My mom said the same thing. But we only have room for a small tree in that little house, so it's just as well if we don't inherit ornaments yet."

Badger unbuttoned his coat. "How many trees are we gettin'?"

"Just Mom's and ours this year," Ryker said. "Normally we need more, but Cody and Faith already cut theirs and the rest want live trees they can plant later."

"Are we usin' that sled I saw?"

"Yep." Ryker came over and grabbed his jacket from the coat tree by the door. "I was about to go hitch up Jake if you want to come."

"Sure do."

"April and I will be down shortly with the cider," Kendra said.

Badger followed Ryker out to the front porch. "What's the cider for?"

"It's something we've done for years. We drink a toast to the tree before we cut it." He pulled on his gloves as they walked toward the barn. "When we were kids, it was warm apple cider. Now it's still warm, but it's the hard stuff."

"You have some cool traditions around here."

"We do, but I'll bet you had some, too."

"Not that I remember. Goin' somewhere else for Christmas is the only tradition that sticks in my head."

"Your folks always went away for the holidays?"

"As far back as I can remember."

"So where are they this year?"

"Biarritz."

"Huh. For how long?"

"I think they're comin' back the thirtieth. They always have a big party on New Year's Eve. That's why I'll be glad to stay here through the first. I'd be expected to go, and everybody would be askin' about my plans."

Ryker shook his head. "What a nightmare for you."

"Yes, sir."

"Listen, you'll need work gloves for this. While I get Jake, go check in the tack room. Should be several extra pairs on a shelf to the right of the door."

Badger found some gloves that fit and went back out as Ryker was hitching the big bay to the sled. "Couldn't y'all just take a truck?"

"Maybe, although the chances of getting stuck make it not the best option. Besides, this is more fun."

"I'll give you that. I've enjoyed this ranchin' experience, Cowboy. I'm obliged to you for invitin' me here."

Ryker glanced at him. "Have you enjoyed it enough to consider staying?"

"I'll admit I'm leanin' in that direction. But that decision would drive the last nail in the casket when it comes to my folks."

"Are you sure about that?"

"I am. If you'd heard them, you would be, too."

"Have you mentioned this option?"

"No reason to. It's not the option they want to hear about."

Ryker shrugged. "Yeah, well, you know them and I don't." He gave Jake a pat and stepped away from the sled. "I did want to ask you about one thing, though, before my mom and April get here."

"What's that?"

"Rumor has it you bought Hayley a big ol' engagement ring."

"I guess Jim's been talkin'."

"No reason for him not to. He didn't think it was a secret since you chose to ask her to marry you while Jim was driving the sleigh." Ryker shoved back his hat. "But I'm asking myself why you did something like that."

"Seemed like I needed to. Her momma expected it."

"So what?"

"If I didn't come up with a ring and propose, she'd think I wasn't serious about marryin' her daughter. The story would start fallin' apart."

"Okay, I suppose I get that, but it's one more complication. Now you have to worry about getting the ring back."

"No, I don't. I want her to keep it."

Ryker's jaw dropped. "*Keep* it? Jim thought it looked really expensive!"

"I don't need the money. And it looks good on her. The stone matches her eyes."

"The stone matches her eyes." Ryker said it slowly. "You're falling for her."

"No, I'm not. That would be stupid."

"Yes, it would." Ryker gazed at him. "Is she falling for you?"

"Why would she do that? I'm pretendin' to be her fiancé because she's not ready to get married and wanted a vacation without bein' set up every five minutes."

"That's what I thought you said the day I picked you up at the airport."

"Well, nothing's changed. She's happy with her job in Denver. If she decides she wants a man in her life, she needs to pick somebody from there." A dull ache worked its way up the back of his neck. Much more of this talk and he'd have a full-blown headache.

"So the two of you are just putting on a show for her mother?"

"Right."

"Apart from the ring you gave her that matches her eyes. The ring you want her to keep."

His jaw tightened. "I'm not fallin' for her, Cowboy."

"I sincerely hope you're not. Because if you do, I see a train wreck in your future."

21

Saving a seat for Badger wasn't going to work. Tables at the Guzzling Grizzly seated four unless two were pushed together to accommodate six.

Hayley watched for Badger to come in with the McGavins. When he arrived, she excused herself and went to meet him. "I can't figure out how we can sit together unless—"

"No problem, darlin'. Let me see what I can do about it." He smiled as his gaze swept over her. "That white sweater makes you look prettier'n a speckled pup."

She rolled her eyes. "Thank you for that, Badger."

"Hang on. I see some tables bein' moved around. I'll be right back." He rejoined his group and gestured to Hayley and the table where her family sat. When he returned, he was all smiles. "We can make room if your folks would like to sit with us."

"All right. Let's ask."

Badger rested his hand on her shoulder as she made her way back to her family. "Sweater's really soft, too," he murmured.

"Cashmere."

"Thought so." He greeted her parents and Luke warmly and invited them over to the McGavin table with enthusiasm. Abandoning their chairs, they followed him over to the large gathering on the far side of the room.

Luke was the only one who didn't know everybody, so after he was introduced and handshakes exchanged, they all settled into a seat. Hayley ended up with Badger on her left and Luke on her right.

Her mom and dad were on the other side of the table but down several seats, talking with Kendra and Jo. Luke struck up a conversation with April, who was on his right. A waitress came and took everyone's order for drinks. The party was on.

Badger looked at her and grinned. "See how that all worked out?"

"It did. Good job. How'd your juggling practice go?"

"Terrible, but they say a bad rehearsal means a good performance."

"I'm sure you'll be great. Even if—"

"Hayley!" Her mother's voice rose over the hum of conversation. "Come down here and show Kendra and Jo your ring!"

The ring. She was so used to it already that she'd forgotten she had it on.

"Ring?" April leaned past Luke. "I didn't hear about that. When did Badger give it to you?"

Hayley's cheeks grew hot. "Yesterday." She pushed back her chair because there was no getting around this display of her engagement ring. She had to do it.

"Yesterday?" April's eyebrows lifted. "This is old news? Badger, shame on you. We chopped down Christmas trees together and I didn't hear about this." She looked at Ryker on her right. "Did you know?"

"Well, I—"

"You did! Both of you knew and didn't say a thing to Kendra and me this afternoon. Is this a pilot's code of silence thing?"

"It wasn't mine to tell," Ryker said.

"Or mine," Badger added. "It's Hayley's ring. She has the say-so about spreadin' the word."

April let out a little *harrumph* of displeasure. "I suppose that's reasonable. You two flyboys are off the hook. Hayley, on your way around the table, let me see, okay? I'm thrilled for you, girlfriend."

Beside her, Ryker looked uncomfortable. "April, anytime you want to talk about—"

"Hey, no, I don't. You and I are still getting reacquainted. We're not ready for rings and such." She took Hayley's hand. "But this one is lovely. A sapphire, right?"

"Yes."

April leaned on the table and engaged Badger again. "Great choice. It matches her eyes."

"I kn—" He coughed. "I'm glad you like it."

"Just so Hayley likes it." April glanced up at her. "But what am I saying? What woman wouldn't want a sapphire that sparkles like a mountain stream in sunlight?"

"I can't imagine." Hayley appreciated the goodwill coming her way, but once she severed the connection with Badger, the outpouring of approval would dry up like a puddle in a heat wave.

She made the obligatory rounds to show everyone the ring. The exercise was illuminating. Four committed McGavin couples were at the table. Of those, only Mandy had a ring, and she was already married to Zane.

Yet Hayley had this knockout of a sapphire. Those who knew the story realized she and Badger hadn't known each other long. She found herself babbling about long engagements, an idea borrowed from her father.

Her mom, though, was in her element. At last she had a daughter who was engaged to be married. When Badger had suggested this subterfuge, Hayley had pictured it as harmless fun to get her through the holidays without a series of mystery dates.

She hadn't envisioned the waves of reaction that would touch so many lives. She'd never perpetrated a hoax in her life, unless she counted the time she'd told Luke that Freddy Krueger was real and would come after him if he didn't share his stash of Milky Ways.

Her progression around the table was painfully slow, but eventually she made it back to her chair beside Badger.

He put his mouth close to her ear. "I'm so sorry. I had no clue."

"I forgot I had it on."

"Your mom didn't."

"No. But it's okay." She took a sip of the beer that had been placed at her seat while she was gone. "It's Christmas. Weird things happen at Christmas."

"They sure have this year."

"Are you calling me a weird happening?"

"No. You're all Christmas cookies and eggnog. The weirdness is on my side. I—never mind. The show is about to start."

Hayley didn't know much about Bryce McGavin other than his recent purchase of the Guzzling Grizzly and his good-natured guitar playing during his family's Yule celebration.

But when he walked out on stage wearing a snow-white Stetson and a red silk shirt, she saw a star in the making. He invited Nicole to join him and she wore a matching Stetson and a green silk shirt.

Each had a guitar slung over their shoulder. They held hands and executed a deep bow to the audience. Then they launched into a rocking rendition of *Winter Wonderland* while a well-designed light show bathed them in swirling snowflakes.

The McGavin contingent went wild and Hayley joined in. She reluctantly admitted that she'd thought of Eagles Nest as a cute little town without much sophistication. Bryce and Nicole had talent and style that would dazzle an audience anywhere.

The show continued with one fantastic act after another. Fire chief Javier Ortega led Trevor McGavin and several other firefighters in a rousing rendition of *God Rest Ye Merry Gentlemen.*

Ellie Mae Stockton, an eighty-something woman Hayley recognized as a clerk from Pills and Pop Drugstore, performed a slinky version of *Santa Baby* that brought down the house.

Her dad was up next. At some point when she wasn't paying attention, he'd changed into green spandex and a red cape. A huge G was emblazoned on his chest. Bryce came out holding up a placard that read *Holy Hilarity, Godman!*

She started giggling before he'd said a single word. Then he started firing one-liners so fast that she barely finished laughing about one before the next one hit. People couldn't drink their beer because sure as the world they'd end up choking on it. At the end of her dad's performance, he pressed his palms together, took a bow and left the stage amid thunderous applause.

When the commotion died down from that, Greg Paladin, owner of Paladin Construction, played a haunting version of *Silent Night* on his harmonica. Then it was Badger, Ryker and Cody's turn.

Badger squeezed her hand. "Wish me luck."

"You'll be awesome." Her attention was glued to the stage as three broad-shouldered cowboys stepped into position with Cody in the middle.

The men each took several deep breaths and flexed their fingers. Then the Trans-Siberian Orchestra's version of *Carol of the Bells* poured from the sound system as red and green plates started flying.

Hayley was mesmerized throughout the song. She focused mostly on Badger but sometimes glanced at the other two. They flipped, spun and tossed those plates with dizzying speed.

It was over way too soon for her. She clapped wildly. Badger, Ryker and Cody returned to the table amid congratulations from everyone.

Once Badger had reclaimed his chair next to hers, she caught his face in both hands and kissed him.

His gaze warmed. "Guess I'll have to put on a juggling demonstration more often." He wiggled his eyebrows. "Maybe even a private one."

"No, that would be selfish. You need to perform for an audience that appreciates talent like yours. That goes for all three of you."

After that, Michael Murphy, co-owner of the bar, stepped away from his duties to sing *Ave Maria* in a stunning Irish tenor. And for the grand finale, the Whine and Cheese Club lined up on stage. They'd ducked into the bathroom earlier to put on their elf costumes. As Sweet Tee's *Let the Jingle Bells Rock* filled the room with rhythmic Christmas spirit, the women let loose with their hip-hop number.

Hayley got a kick out of their loose-limbed rendition but she loved the reaction from Kendra's sons. All four at the table were on their feet, whistling and clapping in time to the dance. The rest of the audience took their cue from the McGavin brothers and rose as a group to urge the women on. Energy flowed through the room in waves of joy.

She glanced back at Badger and his face was alight as he clapped and whistled along with the rest of the men at the table. He was clearly having the time of his life at this party.

The end of the song was greeted with a roar of approval. On impulse, Hayley turned back to Badger and gave him a hug. "Having fun?"

"I love this town," he murmured. "I could live here."

22

Badger had surprised himself by announcing to Hayley that he could live in Eagles Nest. It had been a private thought and he didn't normally say that kind of thing out loud. Luckily she hadn't had time to react. The party had shifted into high gear following the talent show and had continued into the wee hours of the morning.

Just as well that she hadn't had a chance to question him about his remark. He'd bid her a sweet goodnight before she'd left with her folks. The Bennetts traditionally spent Christmas Eve day together, just the four of them.

Hayley had wanted to preserve that. Consequently, Badger wasn't scheduled to see her again until he attended the candlelight service. That was fine with him. He needed time to think.

Kendra had driven him to the Guzzling Grizzly and he'd offered to take the wheel on the way back because she'd looked tired. He, on the other hand, had been wide awake. He'd spent the drive heaping praise on her family and the generous folks of Eagles Nest. She'd listened with a sleepy smile.

By the next morning, he'd made his decision. He texted Ryker and asked for a moment to talk. Ryker invited him over to Olivia's place where he and Trevor were working on April's henhouse in a last-ditch effort to finish it.

When Badger arrived, Olivia's front yard was covered with sawdust. The henhouse, which sat on a canvas tarp, looked about half done. Trevor had built a fancy one for Kendra a few months ago and this one looked as if it would be similar—a miniature Victorian on stilts.

Ryker and Trevor wore ratty old jackets, baseball caps and work gloves. Other than their jeans and boots, they didn't look much like cowboys today.

Ryker handed Trevor a board he'd just cut before walking over to greet Badger. "What's up? Your text sounded urgent."

"It kinda is, but keep workin'. I'd offer to help, but this isn't my area of expertise."

"It's not my strong suit, either." Ryker headed back over to the henhouse and picked up another board. "Trev's the boss man on this deal."

"And how sweet it is, too." Trevor lowered the nail gun he'd been using and turned to grin at Badger. "You here to help?"

"Nah, I'm here to get in the way. Looks good so far."

Trevor lifted his cap, wiped his forehead on his sleeve and repositioned the cap. "It's coming along."

"You goin' to paint it pretty colors like your momma's?"

"Too cold. The wood's been treated so it should hold up until spring. We'll paint then."

"It's better that we aren't going to paint it," Ryker said. "April will want to choose the colors. She'll be happy that it's unpainted."

Badger shoved his hands in the pockets of his jacket. "It's good you know that about her."

"I'd better know it after all the time we've spent together." He turned to Trevor and held up the board. "Two inches off this one, too?"

"Yep. I need five more of those, so just keep cutting."

Ryker motioned to Badger. "You can talk while I'm sawing but you'll have to talk loud."

"No problem." He followed Ryker over to the table saw.

"So what's on your mind?" Ryker turned on the saw.

Badger cleared his throat and yelled it out above the whine of the saw. "I've decided to work with you!"

Ryker turned off the saw and stared at him. "What?"

"I've made my decision. If you still want me to move here, I'd like to fly with you."

Ryker typically wore what guys in the squadron had called his warrior face. But when he was happy, nobody could light up like Cowboy. He lit up now. "That's awesome." His voice was gruff with emotion as he put down the board and stuck out his hand. "Welcome to Badger Air." Then he pulled him into a quick bro hug.

Trevor laid aside his nail gun and came over. "Did I hear right, Badger? You're throwing in with this big lug?"

"Yeah." He couldn't stop grinning. "He needs me. His juggling skills have gone to hell since we broke up the act."

Trevor nodded solemnly, although his mouth twitched. "Good move. I noticed last night he was the weak link."

"Damned if I was! Genius over here bobbled my favorite thrift store find, the plate with the Christmas tree on it. I thought it was done for."

"Nope. I was in full control, whereas if I hadn't acted with consummate skill and dexterity, we would have been vacuuming up the pieces of that red and green platter you almost dropped."

Trevor crossed his arms. "Clearly both of you morons need some serious practice before next year's show."

"They'll do it again next Christmas?" Badger hadn't counted on that. Talk about frosting on the cake. He'd loved that show.

"Definitely," Trevor said. "Maybe you missed it because you were playing kissy-face with your fiancée, but Bryce announced it as everybody was leaving. Looks like we've got us a new tradition in Eagles Nest."

"That's great. Especially seein' as how it was that show that jumpstarted me thinkin' that I need to make the move."

"I can see how that would happen. Last night was epic. Eagles Nest at its best." Trevor punched him lightly on the shoulder. "It'll be good having you around, Badger."

"Thanks. But I'm gonna take off now and let you both get back to work." He turned to leave.

"Hang on a sec." Ryker glanced at his brother. "I'll be back in a minute. I have a few questions for Badger."

"Sure thing. Now that we're this far along, I'm not worried. We'll make it."

"Hey, Cowboy, no need to iron out the details now. We can do that later."

"This won't take long. I'll just mosey over to the truck with you." He fell into step beside him. "I take it you've acclimated to the cold?"

"Aw, that was just a chicken-shit excuse."

"'Cause you couldn't see yourself disappointing your folks a second time?"

"Yes, sir."

"So what changed?"

"Remember what I said about badger bein' my spirit animal?"

"Sure."

"I just took that guy's word for what it meant, but last night after I got home I looked it up online to double check."

"Let me guess. It said you were a royal pain in the butt."

"That's about the gist of it. Badger goes his or her own way. Doesn't worry about what others think. When I enlisted, I acted like Badger. When I came back, I quit bein' myself. It's time I got back to bein' Badger again. If my folks get upset, if they decide to quit talkin' to me on account of me doin' what's right for me, that's on them."

Respect gleamed in Ryker's gaze. "Good plan."

"Thanks. I like it."

"What about Hayley?"

"I'm still thinkin' about Hayley."

"Oh, shit. Here it comes."

"But see, I've got direction, now. I know where I'm goin'."

"Right off a cliff."

"Maybe not."

"She still lives in Denver."

"I know. But that's not Timbuktu. And I'll have a plane."

"*We'll* have a plane, and it won't be available to fly your sorry ass to—"

"We'll each have a plane."

"Regardless." Ryker sighed. "But I'm wasting my breath. I saw how you looked at her last night. Just take it slow, okay? Don't say anything stupid or incriminating."

"Like what?"

"If I have to spell it out...oh, what the hell. You're gonna do what you're gonna do. And if you crash and burn, I'll just get you drunk and put you back together again." Ryker smiled and gripped his shoulder. "It'll be good flying with you again, Badger."

"Same here, Cowboy." Now that he'd made the decision, he couldn't imagine why it had taken him so long. This was his path. Always had been.

In Atlanta, he'd get to be a lawyer but that was about it. Oh, he'd also get to be Thaddeus Livingston Calhoun the Third. His folks had refused to call him Badger.

Out here he'd established that Badger was his name. He had both a commuter airline and a raptor nursery named after him. He had the freedom to be a cowboy, a pilot and a juggler. As time went on, he might find more designations to tack on.

After saying goodbye to Ryker, he drove back to town and parked on Main Street. Eagles Nest had looked inviting before, but now that he'd decided to live here, the place charmed the living daylights out of him. The holiday decorations sparkled brighter and the shop windows glowed with extra good cheer.

He stopped for lunch at the Eagles Nest Diner because he'd never eaten there and he wanted to check out the menu. The Guzzling Grizzly would always be his first choice, but it didn't serve breakfast and sometimes he might want to go out for a stack of pancakes and some eggs over easy.

The subject of breakfast naturally took him straight to the subject of Hayley. Christmas was tomorrow and he didn't have a gift for her. The ring didn't count because she'd known about it.

But what to get her? More jewelry? No, that lacked imagination. Wait, she'd been enamored of the collectibles store. After finishing his lunch, he walked down there.

The shop was a cheerful clutter of vintage jewelry, classic board games, jigsaw puzzles, fancy teapots and Montana memorabilia. Badger strolled the aisles until he found the book section. Several Hardy Boys mysteries sat next to a row of Black Stallion books.

"May I help you?"

He glanced down at a small woman with white hair, kind eyes and a great smile. "I surely hope so."

Her smile widened. "You're Southern."

"I am."

"I have a really nice copy of *Gone with the*—"

"That's good to know, but that's not what I'm lookin' for."

"Of course you're not. That was a knee-jerk reaction. What *are* you looking for?"

"I'm not sure. I want a gift for someone who came in here two days ago with her momma. She's blonde, about so tall." He held his hand under his chin.

"Could you be a little more specific? I've had a lot of people in my shop this past month and that describes several of them."

"She turned thirty this year and she's real pretty."

She gave him a sympathetic glance. "Doesn't narrow it down much."

"Her momma lives here. She's a weddin' planner. Hayley, her daughter who's visitin' for the the holidays, bought a Black Stallion book for her brother."

"Bingo! Virginia Bennett and her daughter. Hayley got *The Black Stallion Returns.* She seemed interested in the series. Did you want to buy her one of those?"

"Probably not. If she's collecting them she might already have whatever I picked. Did she look at anything else?"

"Let me think." She tapped her lower lip. "Yes, she did! *The Secret Garden* by Frances Hodgson Burnett. I have a 1911 First Edition in excellent condition but it's pricey."

"I'd like to buy it."

She blinked. "But you don't even know how much—"

"Doesn't matter."

"All righty, then. You just made this a very Merry Christmas, indeed." She fished a key from her pocket, opened the case and took out an old-fashioned hardback. It had no paper dustcover. Just the book. "Would you like it gift-wrapped?"

"Yes, ma'am."

"Would you like me to do a tap-dance while I wrap it?"

He chuckled. "Do you know how?"

"No, but for this kind of money, I could fake it."

"That fancy paper's good enough."

"Hayley's a lucky lady."

"No, ma'am. I'm the lucky one." Maybe. Time would tell.

Ten minutes later, the wrapped book tucked inside his jacket to protect it, he left the shop. Now that he had a gift, he had to decide when and how to give it to her.

He wanted it to be elegant. Showing up at her folks' house on Christmas morning and slipping his gift in with the others beneath the tree didn't seem like the way to go.

This wasn't a Christmas gift to be opened while her family looked on. Instead he'd give it to her in a more intimate setting, maybe even tonight when they were alone in the B&B. And like Ryker had said, he'd try not to say anything stupid or incriminating.

23

Hayley had loved having private time with her family so they could do all the nostalgic things that were a part of a Bennett Christmas – tree decorating, board games and favorite holiday cartoons.

Her snowball fight with Luke in the backyard had been like old times. The light Christmas Eve supper of vegetable soup and homemade rolls that they had every year tasted as good as it always had. But she'd missed Badger.

After going nearly twenty-four hours without seeing him, she kept peeking out the window, impatient for him to arrive. She'd already informed her family that after the service she and Badger would be taking a drive to see the lights. All three had looked as if they didn't believe a word of it.

It didn't matter. The charade she and Badger had cooked up gave her carte blanche to disappear to an undisclosed location and cuddle with her fiancé tonight. She'd worn another cashmere sweater, this one a pale blue with a cowl neck, because he'd mentioned the softness of her white one the night before.

He pulled into the drive right on time. Her dad had already walked over to the church to make sure everything was set up.

She grabbed her parka. "Mom! Luke! He's here."

"I'm ready." Her brother exited his bedroom wearing the denim sheepskin coat he'd brought on this trip.

She should have guessed something was up with him when she'd seen that coat. It was like one he used to have when he was in high school, back when he thought of himself as a cowboy.

College had changed all that and he'd started wearing topcoats. He looked handsome no matter what, but she liked the blue denim best. It was more Luke.

"Me, too." Her mom came out of the master bedroom pulling on her bright red parka. She paused at the end of the hallway to look at Hayley and Luke. "You guys are beautiful, you know that?"

Hayley's throat tightened at the love shining in her mother's eyes. "You, too, Mom."

"You're both knockouts." Luke spread his arms wide. "Group hug."

She and her mom exchanged a look and rushed him. They nearly sent him sprawling.

Hayley was still laughing when she went to answer the door. Seeing Badger standing there gave her a rush of pleasure. "Hi!" She stepped back so he could come in.

He grinned. "Hi, yourself." He leaned down to give her a quick kiss before facing Luke and her mom. "Hey, y'all. Ready to go?"

"Let's do it." Luke grabbed his new cowboy hat, another indication he was moving on from his day job.

"Hayley, you and Badger go on ahead," her mom said. "Luke and I will lock up and follow behind you."

"Okay." Hayley zipped her parka and went out the door Badger held open for her.

Once they were down the steps, he took her hand. "You looked happy when you opened the door."

"I was. I am."

"Good day?"

"Yep. How about you?"

"Great day. What'd y'all do?"

"Played games, had a snowball fight, watched *A Garfield Christmas*. How about you?"

"Walked around town quite a bit."

"Alone or with people?"

"Alone. Tried out the diner. Ever eaten there?"

"A few times. It's cozy. But I'm surprised you weren't out at the ranch with Kendra and everybody."

"I had a couple of things to take care of and I felt like walkin' through town."

She was missing something. "Why?"

"I'll tell you about it later." He squeezed her hand. "When we're lookin' at Christmas lights."

Just the mention of that was enough to get her hot. She took a calming breath. "You have both keys, right?"

"In my pocket."

"Okay." She took another deep breath. "I'm going to think about something else, now."

He squeezed her hand again. "Me, too, darlin'. Me, too."

Soft organ music greeted them as they stepped inside the church. Badger took off his hat and unbuttoned his coat as they were each given an unlit candle. Graceful tapers flickered on the altar, casting muted light over pine boughs and holly. Sprays of pine and holly had been attached to the end of each wooden pew. Hayley had always associated the fragrance of beeswax and pine with Christmas Eve.

"Sure is pretty," Badger murmured.

"I love this little church." She took charge of the candles while he helped her out of her parka and took off his coat. "The stained glass is even prettier during the day."

"It reminds me of one I saw in Switzerland."

So he'd been to Switzerland. But she didn't know when or why. And now wasn't the time to ask such questions, either.

"Where should we sit?"

"Up front," Luke said as he came in behind them and took off his jacket. "Dad always reserves a spot for us."

Badger turned to him. "For me, too?"

"Absolutely." Her mom patted his shoulder. "I hope you didn't feel left out today, but Hayley said—"

"Today was for y'all." He helped her out of her coat. "I'm glad you had that time."

Her mother beamed at him. "You're a nice person, Badger. Now everybody scoot up there. We're blocking the way."

In the front pew, the guys sat on either side of the women so Hayley ended up with Badger on one side and her mom on the other.

Her mom leaned over and whispered in her ear. "I don't care what your dad says. Badger is perfect. Don't wait too long."

"Um..."

"Can't you just picture walking down the aisle of this church?"

She hadn't even considered it, but thanks to her mom's comment, she now had that image in her mind. When and if she married someone, this was the fairytale church she'd choose for the ceremony. Her dad would perform the service. Her mom and Luke would walk her down the aisle.

The man who'd be waiting for her at the end of that aisle was anybody's guess, though. Badger was sexy as hell, great to look at and fun to be with, but who was he, really? She had no idea. He'd confided almost nothing of a personal nature.

Yet his warmth and solid presence beside her was nice, very nice. When he laced his strong fingers through hers, she was tempted to weave all kinds of fantasies.

But they wouldn't be based in reality. He was an actor who'd agreed to play a part. He was very good at playing it, but she'd be a fool to start believing in the fantasy.

Her mom leaned over again. "I still think next week we should plan a trip to Bozeman so we can—whoops, it's starting."

Saved by the choir. The organ music swelled, her dad came out wearing his robes, and the choir filed down the aisle holding flickering electric candles as they sang *O Come All Ye Faithful.*

With music filling the church, she almost missed Badger's soft sigh. She put her head close to his. "You okay?"

"Never better." He lifted her hand and kissed her fingertips. Her ring gleamed in the light from the passing candles. "Never better."

She didn't know what to make of it. Any of it. His solo walk through town, his itch to try the diner's food, his sigh of what must be contentment.

Whatever was going on with him, he certainly liked the service. He sang enthusiastically with the rest of the congregation and listened with rapt attention to everything her dad had to say.

She did the same, because she loved the music at this time of year and her dad sure did know how to move a crowd. He never went for laughs on Christmas Eve. He went all in for love, though. She was always proud to be his kid, but never more than on Christmas Eve.

As usual, her mom got teary-eyed. Hayley put her candle in her lap so she could reach over and squeeze her mom's hand. That was how she finished up the service, with one hand captured by Badger and the other giving love to her mother.

Luke had their mom's other hand. The two of them had tag-teamed this event for years. Their dad would be awesome leading the service, their mom would be overcome with pride and love, and Hayley and Luke would give her support.

Badger had never been a part of the scenario before, but somehow he seemed to fit. Then the ushers came around to light the candles of the person on the end of the row. That was Badger. He seemed thrilled about it.

He turned to her. "Merry Christmas, Hayley." Touching his candle to hers, he smiled. "I love this."

"Merry Christmas, Badger. I love it, too." She swiveled around to light her mom's candle, who then lit Luke's. The significance of one person sharing their light with another had always touched her. Now she was a little choked up.

Her dad always ended the service with everyone singing *Silent Night.* This one was acapella. Only the voices of the choir and the congregation rose into the rafters of the little church. It was her favorite part.

The music ended and her father gave the final blessing. Candles were blown out and everyone filed out of the church, voices subdued as they held onto the spiritual high of joining together on Christmas Eve.

Badger, usually so talkative, was quiet on the walk back. When they reached his truck, he hugged her mom and shook hands with Luke. Then he helped her in, and in no time at all they were on the road, bound for the B&B.

She couldn't gauge his mood. "Did you like it?"

"Oh, Hayley, it was wonderful. I never knew a Christmas Eve could be like that."

"Your folks didn't go to church on Christmas Eve?"

"We might have a few times. I remember Switzerland, for sure. But that service wasn't in English and it was...different."

"It sounds like you weren't home much for Christmas."

"Never. But it doesn't matter."

"Of course it matters. If you've never spent a Christmas at home, that's—"

"Not what I want to talk about. I've just had a memorable Christmas Eve and I want to hold onto that for now."

"Okay, sure." He had a point. This wasn't a good time to dig into painful childhood memories. They'd carved out a couple of hours to be together. No sense spoiling their interlude with unpleasant subjects.

He captured her hand. "I do have a few things to tell you about, but if you wouldn't mind too much, I'd like to make love to you first."

"I wouldn't mind. I wouldn't mind at all."

24

Badger hoped to hell he wouldn't say anything stupid or incriminating tonight, but he'd had a startling glimpse into his future while sitting next to Hayley in church. And he couldn't imagine that future without her in it.

On the other hand, Eagles Nest was his home, now, and Hayley didn't live here. Her folks did, though, and that was a start. He couldn't predict how everything would turn out, but now he had two goals—settle himself in Eagles Nest and turn this pretend situation with Hayley into something real. It was a tall order. He didn't kid himself about that.

In the meantime, he had Hayley all to himself for the next little while. He'd make the most of that opportunity.

The B&B was dark except for a porch light and a couple of electric candle arrangements in the two front windows. Path lights guided them up to the door.

Badger let go of Hayley's hand so he could unlock the front door.

"Slipping in after hours feels so..."

"Outrageous?"

"Yes!"

"Great, isn't it?"

She laughed. "It is great. Especially for a minister's daughter."

"Try bein' the son of Thaddeus Livingston Calhoun the Second." Once they were inside the dimly lit foyer, he turned and engaged both top and bottom locks, while she crept quickly up the stairs of the silent house.

He followed, taking two steps to her one and unbuttoning his coat as he climbed. He was right behind her when she opened the door to their room. The room was dark, but moonlight shone through the window.

Walking in, she turned back to him. "The moon's so beautiful," she murmured. "Let's leave the lights off."

"Whatever you want, darlin'." He closed the door and tossed his hat onto the nearest bedpost.

"I want you out of these clothes." She closed the gap between them and pushed aside the lapels of his jacket.

"And I want you out of yours." He wrapped her in his arms. "But I can't seem to stop kissin' you."

"Then don't stop." She rose on her tiptoes and brushed her mouth over his as she began unsnapping his shirt. "We'll work it out."

She was right about that. Somehow they managed to keep on kissing each other as they got rid of every blessed thing they were wearing except for his boots. He leaned against the bedpost to pull those off and then they were back to kissing again while she shoved down his jeans and briefs.

When she finished that, she began touching him in ways that he loved but wouldn't be able to tolerate for long. He lifted his mouth from hers. "You're playin' with fire."

"I know." Her voice was low and husky as she stroked his cock. "It's fun."

"I'm not denyin' that." He gasped as she squeezed gently. "But the fun will be over quick." He wrapped his hand around her fingers. "I've been missin' you. Which means I've built up a head of steam."

She chuckled softly. "Can I play later, after you've let off some steam?"

Her suggestion nearly made him come. "Yes, ma'am, you surely can." He sucked in air. "Just turn me loose for the time bein'."

"Okay." She gave him one last squeeze. "Meet you in bed."

"You know it." His heart thumped hard and fast as he grabbed his jeans off the floor and pulled a condom out of the pocket. His hands shook while he opened the wrapper and rolled on the condom. *Easy, Calhoun. Easy.*

But this time wasn't like the others they'd shared. Now he knew what was at stake. He wasn't just enjoying amazing sex with a beautiful lady. He was about to make love to the woman he hoped would share his life.

She didn't know that and if he followed Ryker's advice, he wouldn't say anything about it tonight. He turned back to the bed and his breath caught.

An angel lay in bed waiting for him. Moonlight touched her hair and body, creating a glorious mix of pale beauty and seductive shadows. He was transfixed.

"Badger?"

"I'm just lookin' my fill." He took a shaky breath. "And thinkin' I'm one lucky SOB."

"You're making me blush."

"And you're makin' me crazy." He climbed onto the bed and moved over her. "Damn. I'm blockin' the moonlight."

"I can still see it." She stroked the side of his face. "Right here. I've never made love in the moonlight before."

"Me, either."

She slid her arms around him. "That makes it special."

"Everything about you is special." Leaning down, he kissed her gently. "Merry Christmas, Hayley."

"Merry Christmas, Badger."

He loved her slowly at first, wanting to savor the pleasure of this intimate connection that had been perfect from the beginning. But he couldn't keep a lid on his response when she tightened around him, when her soft whimpers turned to moans of pleasure.

His blood ran hot as he thrust deep, coaxing her to let go. When she did, when she pressed her hand to her mouth to stifle her cries of release, fierce joy poured through him. He rode the wave of her climax to his and swallowed the roar of triumph he so longed to turn loose.

Sinking down against her warmth, he kept his weight on his forearms. He didn't want to crush her when she was trying to catch her breath. But he rested his cheek against her shoulder.

They were so good together, so damned good. They were meant for each other. It had to work out for them. It just had to.

Reaching up, she combed her fingers through his hair. "I liked that," she murmured. "Making love in the moonlight."

"Me, too." Understatement of the century. *Like* didn't begin to cover it.

"Let's leave the light off a little longer, okay?"

"Works for me." Telling her about his plans in the dark sounded nice, intimate. He eased away from her. "I'll be back."

"I'm counting on it."

After disposing of the condom, he got into bed and stretched out on his side.

She rolled to face him. "Did we ever figure out how we'd work things tomorrow?"

"How do you want to work it?" He stroked her hip. "Your call."

"Not really." She snuggled closer. "You're staying at the ranch. After seeing how they operate, I'll bet they'll have a big gathering tomorrow."

"They will. Kendra said everybody gets together in the morning after they feed the animals and they exchange gifts. Then they scatter to do their own thing until dinner that night."

"You probably want to be there both times."

"I want to be wherever you are."

"Well, we open presents first thing, eat a quick breakfast, and go to church. The big meal for us is in the middle of the day, so that might be the best time for you to come over."

"I'll do that but I also want to go to church with you in the mornin'."

"Well, okay, if you think you can make it. Mom and Dad would be thrilled."

"I'll make it." He slipped his arm around her waist. "In fact, I'll probably be goin' on a regular basis."

"What do you mean?"

"That's what I planned on tellin' you. I've decided I'm goin' to fly with Ryker. I'm movin' to Eagles Nest."

"You *are*?" She scooted back a little. "I thought you were worried you couldn't take the weather?"

"I can take the weather, especially when I have so much goin' for me here. Flyin' with Ryker is the main thing, but I want to get back to ridin' again. I might volunteer at Zane's raptor rescue, too. He named his raptor nursery after me. I don't think I told you that."

"You didn't, but why would he—wait, I can guess. You made a big donation."

"Not huge, but—"

"Must have been substantial if he named something after you."

"I guess he thought it was a lot. Oh, and since I'm movin' here, I can plan on bein' in next year's talent show at the Guzzling Grizzly. I also think your dad's church is great, so I—"

"This all sounds wonderful, and I'm happy for you because you seem happy."

"I am happy." He gave her a squeeze. "Especially right this minute."

"But...the thing is, you moving here creates a slight complication."

He took a deep breath. "I know." This was the part he hadn't worked through, yet. Except there was an obvious solution.

"I mean, it might be okay if we can pull off that friendly breakup you were talking about."

"I suppose." This would be the time Ryker would advise him to shut up. But it might be the perfect time to say something. "What if we...well, what if we didn't break up?"

She went very still. "What are you saying?"

Her tone wasn't very encouraging, but he pushed on. "We get along well, so why should we break up? Why does anyone have to find out about—"

"Oh, Badger." She eased out of his arms and sat up. "Think about it. Everyone except Ryker believes we're engaged to be married. And we're not."

"What's so bad about them believin' that?" He sat up, too, and faced her, although her back was to the moonlight so her face was in shadow.

"For a short time I could live with it because it meant I wouldn't have a bunch of awkward dates this Christmas. But to keep lying about our situation...I can't."

"What if we're not exactly lyin'?"

Her breath quickened. "I don't know what you mean."

"I'm crazy about you, Hayley. And I think you like me a little bit, too. I don't see why we can't just go on like we've been doin'."

She didn't speak right away. When she did, she sounded as if she might be choosing her words carefully. "Like I said, we're not being straight with people and that would bother me. The engagement isn't real."

"What if we make it real?"

The silence stretched between them. "What are you suggesting?"

"That we get engaged."

More silence. "Engaged to be married?"

"It would solve everything." When she didn't answer, he got a little worried. "Wouldn't it?"

"No." She sounded almost sad.

"Why not?"

"Because people, specifically my mother, would expect us to get married. And I can't marry you."

"Because you live in Denver?"

"No, because I don't know who you are."

"Sure you do! We've spent all kinds of time together the last few days."

"And you've told me almost nothing about yourself."

"That can't be right. You know where I'm from, that I've been in the Air Force..." He searched for something to add.

"Those are broad strokes and not many of them. I kept hoping you'd tell me that your dad is a prominent lawyer and that you went to Georgetown."

"How'd you know that?"

"My folks looked you up online."

"Oh."

She left the bed and walked over to the wall switch by the door.

"What are you doing?"

"Shedding some light on the situation." She flipped the switch and the bedside lamps came on. She started gathering her clothes.

He blinked in the sudden glare. "I guess I should have told you more."

"Before we started coming to this B&B, it didn't really matter." She pulled on her clothes. "But after that, yes, I wished you'd open up. When you didn't, I assumed you still thought of this as a temporary arrangement."

"That's changed."

"Maybe in your mind, but you're still a mystery to me. Other than those tidbits online, I know nothing about your childhood or your parents."

"Yes, you do! I told you they wouldn't let me watch TV and I had a tutor before I started school."

"And how did you feel about that?"

"It's not important, now. It's in the past."

"It's *extremely* important! But the fact that you just said it's not tells me so much." Her voice gentled. "I'm sorry, Badger. I'm not sure how you envisioned this working out, but it's plain to me that it won't. The sooner we pull the plug, the easier it will be on both of us."

He couldn't believe it. This couldn't be happening. Not after all they'd—

"Please get dressed. I want you to take me home."

25

The silent ride home was awful. By the time Badger pulled up in front of the parsonage, Hayley felt sick to her stomach. But she remembered to pull off the ring. "Here."

"I'm not takin' that. It's yours. Stay there. I want to help you out."

She almost climbed out anyway, but in the end, she let him hand her down because that was so important to him. She considered dropping the ring in the cup holder, but he might not see it there and this was Kendra's truck.

She couldn't just leave it in the truck and hope he'd find it. *He bought it because it matched your eyes.* Nope. Couldn't think about that now. She tucked it in her pocket.

After he helped her get down, he continued to hold her hand. "Hayley, I've made a mess of this. I can see that. But if you'll just—"

"Badger, you're a sweet guy. I wish you well." Her throat tightened. "But this charade is over." She avoided looking at him as she drew her hand away and hurried down the walkway. Thankfully he didn't follow her.

But memories did. Badger hurrying to her defense at the airport. His grin of delight when her dad made a joke. The sparkle in his eyes when he called her darlin'. His tender expression during the candle lighting ceremony...

She'd hurt him. She'd never forget the way his broad shoulders had slumped when she'd asked him to take her home. Their affair had to end, but dear God, why couldn't it have been...what was his word? Amicable. Instead the pain sliced and twisted through her and likely was torturing him, too.

She slept very little and woke up with a hangover. Had to be an emotional hangover because she hadn't had a drop to drink. But Christmas morning was important in this house so she dragged herself out of bed.

Her ring lay on the bedside table. If she appeared in the living room without it, her mom would notice. Painful though it was to put it back on her finger, she did. It seemed to weigh a hundred pounds.

She managed to keep up the pretense through the opening of presents, but she ached as if she had the flu. She pictured Badger at the ranch surrounded by McGavins in celebration mode. No doubt he was soldiering through it like she was.

She almost expected to see him at church that morning because he'd said he'd be there. If he showed up, she'd conclude that he'd decided to keep up appearances even though she'd shot him down. But he didn't come.

She adjusted her thinking accordingly. If she explained that Badger felt obligated to spend

Christmas Day with the McGavins, that might buy her some time before she had to drop her bomb. Because drop it she must. With luck she could hold off until the twenty-sixth.

The midday Christmas dinner table was loaded with all the food she loved, yet she could barely choke it down. Then came the inevitable question.

Her mom turned to her. "When's Badger coming over, sweetheart? You haven't said."

"Oh, you know, he really felt he should spend the day with Ryker and the McGavin family."

"You mean not see you at all on Christmas?" Her mother looked dismayed. "After getting better acquainted with Kendra at the talent show, I can't believe she'd expect Badger to—"

"She doesn't. It's Badger who thinks that he should be there."

Luke frowned. "But he's engaged to you. Christmas is a big deal, especially when you're newly engaged. Did he ask you to join him over there?"

"No, but it's not important. We'll have plenty of Christmases together and the McGavins were the ones who invited him to—"

"Look, sis, if you're not a priority now, when will you be? I'm not liking this decision of Badger's. I'm not liking it at all. He could run over here for an hour or two, at least. Or come get you and take you out to the ranch."

"Luke does have a point," her dad said. "I'm a little disappointed in Badger, myself."

"Please don't be." Hearing him maligned cut deeper than she'd expected. "This is not his fault. It's mine."

"Yours?" Her mother stared at her. "How can it be your fault?"

"I...the thing is...I broke up with him last night."

Silence reigned at the table for several seconds.

Her mom had gone very pale. "But you're still wearing his ring."

"I'll get it back to him. Last night it would have been awkward." Her stomach flipped as the emotions from that horrible ride home flooded through her.

"Oh, well, then!" Her mom waved a hand as if dismissing the problem. "It's just a lovers' spat. Give it time. You'll realize how much you love each other and everything will be fine."

Hayley started to agree with her. Maybe she could still salvage Christmas Day. Before she could say anything, her mother barreled on.

"Hayley, you should call him. I'll bet he's as upset as you are. Go for a drive. Take a walk. Your father and I have sorted out so many issues with a good long walk. Isn't that right, Warren?"

"Yes, but this might not be the same situ—"

"It's not that simple." Hayley took a deep breath. Should she do this? Should she admit the truth and wreck what remained of Christmas Day? Then she looked at Luke, who was so trusting and so willing to be her champion no matter what.

She didn't like fooling her parents, but she *really* didn't like fooling Luke. Ever since she'd lied to him about Freddie Krueger, she'd told him the truth. Until now.

Taking another deep breath, she plunged in. "Look, I'm so sorry. So very sorry. But the thing is, Badger and I were never a couple in the first place."

Her dad sat up straighter. "What? What are you saying, Hayley?"

"I lied, Dad." The admission was difficult enough. Her father's crestfallen expression nearly did her in. "I'm so sorry."

"Hayley?" Her mom stared at her in shock. "What do you mean, sweetheart?"

"Badger and I..." She almost couldn't say it. "We met for the first time in the Denver airport."

"Months ago, right?" Her mother looked so hopeful.

"No. Last week."

Luke groaned. Clearly he'd made the leap.

But her mom wouldn't want to. "I don't understand. If you only met last week, then how—"

"We made it all up, Mom."

Her mother pressed a hand to her chest. "Why?"

"Because..." She swallowed. "Because I didn't want to go through another Christmas of fixups."

As the realization dawned, her mother's face crumpled and she began to cry. Her dad crouched by her chair and comforted her while

Luke went for tissues and Bailey's. Everyone took some Bailey's in their coffee except her dad, who had another sermon to give. Only Hayley and her mom grabbed tissues.

Eventually they moved into the living room, but her mother continued to sob. "I drove you to this? How can I ever forgive myself?"

Hayley's dad sat beside her on the couch with his arm around her shoulders. Hayley and Luke commandeered a position on the floor at her feet and told her how much they loved her, even if she was a pain in the butt sometimes.

"I promise to do better," her mom said between bouts of blowing her nose. "This is a wakeup call."

Luke patted her knee. "I hate seeing you cry, but...I'm sort of relieved we're talking about this. I've considered moving to Eagles Nest."

"Oh, Luke, I would love that! So would your father!"

"And you wouldn't try to marry me off? I've seen what Hayley's gone through and she's not even living here."

That brought more tears. "I've driven my children away! Warren, this is terrible!"

"But correctible, now that everything's out in the open." Her dad smiled. "Right, kids?"

"Right, Dad," Luke said.

Hayley turned to him. "You really might move here?"

"If I'm not afraid of being hounded into marriage, you bet. It's a great town. You should move, too. Then the Bennetts can all be together again."

It was a wild idea, but an appealing one. It had nothing to do with Badger Calhoun, of course... "But I love my job."

Luke grinned at her. "But you love us more, right?"

"Yeah, I do. And April mentioned that I could become a traveling consultant and get Badger Air to fly me around." Ryker would fly her, though. Not Badger. Except...she would likely run into him if she moved here. And, oh, dear God, she wanted to run into him. When she got right down to it, never seeing Badger Calhoun again was a bleak prospect indeed. But there were issues. Big issues.

"Let's check out the possibilities." Her dad got up, retrieved his laptop and sat beside his wife again. "Searching online doesn't seem quite right on Christmas, but this is a family emergency."

Luke winked at Hayley. "I think God would approve."

"So do I, son. And what do I have here?" He gazed at the screen and flipped the laptop around so Hayley could see it. "We have elder care going on all over the state. You could be your own boss instead of working for someone else."

"I could."

"Broaden your reach. Maybe travel to underserved areas."

"You're right. Older people live in rural areas, and they may not have access to—"

"Exactly! It's a brilliant idea, sis." Luke smiled at her. "I'm inspired just hearing about it."

Her mom blew her nose again. "If you two kids are willing to trust me enough to move here, I won't let you down. I had no idea my behavior was keeping you away."

Hayley glanced up at her mother. "You meant well, Mom. I know you love us."

Her mother looked at her and swallowed. "More than you can imagine." She held her gaze. "I need to say something, and it's not because I'm matchmaking."

"That's good to hear."

"Because of your sweet father, I know what love looks like. You and Badger weren't totally faking it."

* * *

People said war was hell, and Badger wouldn't argue that. But when a guy had been kicked to the curb on Christmas Eve by the first woman he'd ever proposed to, the first one he'd truly pictured spending his life with, that was damned hellish, too. Being surrounded by cheerful people on Christmas morning added another heaping of awfulsauce. He kept his smile pasted on as best he could.

Last night he'd questioned whether he should scrap his plan to move to Eagles Nest. This morning he'd figured out that would be a bonehead move. Cutting off his nose to spite his face made no sense whatsoever.

But part of his excitement for taking the job with Ryker and moving here had involved Hayley. She might not have chosen to live here, but then again, once she didn't have to worry about her momma's matchmaking, she might have considered it.

Maybe not right away, and he'd been willing to carry on long distance if necessary, but a life with her in this little town had seemed possible. Remorse for the sorry state of things welled up in him, a toxic soup of self-blame. Cowboy had told him not to say anything stupid in the heat of the moment. He'd gone and done exactly that.

Now she didn't want anything to do with him and he didn't know how to repair the damage. And there could be collateral damage, too, depending on what Hayley had told her folks. He didn't want to lose her, but he also didn't want to lose her family.

She wouldn't paint him as the bad guy. She was too kind for that. After the holidays, he'd attend a service at that beautiful little church and find out if her folks were speaking to him.

Keeping in touch with them was a good thing all by itself because he liked them so much. But they were also a link to Hayley. He might have to play a long game, but he wasn't giving up.

Evidently he'd managed to hide his misery from the McGavins during the Christmas morning festivities and he was glad about that. He hadn't expected gifts but got some, anyway. It was almost like they'd known all along he'd choose to stay, because he got a ton of gloves, scarves and even a pair of snow boots.

Everyone had exclaimed over his gifts of Chihuly blown glass paperweights that he'd found on a visit to the Atlanta Botanical Garden. No two were alike and he loved that. He only wished he'd brought enough to give Warren and Virginia one since they'd visited the city twice and likely had toured that garden.

Eventually all the gifts had been opened and the living room was strewn with ribbons, paper, bags and boxes. Nothing like the tidy Christmas mornings in foreign settings that he was used to. This was more like it.

It cheered him up some that he could look forward to another Christmas morning like this next year. Ryker had spread the word that he'd be moving to Eagles Nest and everyone had made a point of saying how glad they were. He felt wanted. Well, here, at least.

As people started picking up the wrappings and packing up to leave, Kendra glanced at him. "When are you due over at the Bennetts?"

"I, um, I won't be goin' over there today, after all."

"Not even for a little while?"

"No, ma'am." He hadn't figured out an appropriate time to break the news but this didn't seem like it. "She needs to be with her family."

Kendra looked puzzled. "But you're her family, now, too."

"Well, I—"

"It's okay." Kendra's voice took on a soothing tone, as if she'd guessed something wasn't right and he didn't want to elaborate. "Never mind. I'm glad we have you to ourselves today."

He let out a breath. "Thank you, ma'am. I'm mighty glad to be here."

The leave-taking continued until Kendra, Ryker and April were the only ones left.

Kendra asked April to come into the kitchen to consult on some item for tonight's dinner and Ryker moseyed over to where Badger was picking up the last bits of paper.

"Let's you and me take a walk."

"Don't you and April need to get on home?"

"We're in no rush."

"But—"

"Get your coat and hat, soldier. Clearly you've screwed the pooch and we need to talk."

26

Hayley hadn't expected to hear from Badger. She hadn't left any room for negotiation when she'd shot him down. And she didn't hear from him. But three days after Christmas she got a text from Ryker asking if she'd have coffee with him at the Pie in the Sky Bakery.

Just you? she texted back.

Just me. I'm not into ambushing folks.

She agreed to meet him that afternoon at two-thirty. Although he'd said Badger wouldn't be there, her heart still raced as she parked and walked into the fragrant shop.

Normally when she drove past, the place was bustling, but evidently this was the bakery's slow time. Only one customer roamed in front of the pastry case choosing goodies from the tempting array behind the curved glass.

Ryker sat in the small seating area that included four tables with two chairs each. Both the table and the chair looked a little small for him. He stood when she walked toward him. "Thanks for meeting me."

"Does this have to do with Badger?"

"Yes, ma'am." He helped her off with her coat and hooked it on a nearby vintage coatrack. "If that's a problem, though, we don't have to talk about him. We can just have some coffee and maybe a slice of pie."

She sat on the chair opposite him. "It's not a problem. But is he out at the ranch? You said you don't do ambushes but I—"

"You don't have to worry that he'll come strolling in here. He's in Atlanta."

"Oh!" Maybe she'd secretly wanted to be ambushed. "Did he change his mind about moving here?" She didn't care for that possibility, either.

"No, ma'am. He just went back to gather his stuff." Ryker glanced up when a woman with short, curly brown hair arrived. He gave her a smile. "Judging from Mom's description, you must be Abigail Summers."

"I am."

"I'm Ryker McGavin and this is Hayley Bennett."

"Pleased to meet you both. What can I get for you on this chilly afternoon?"

"Coffee for now, and maybe some pie. I've been wanting to come in here ever since tasting that Yule log Mom got. Spectacular."

"I have another one in the back that's not spoken for."

"You do? Then I'll take it home to April." He looked over at Hayley. "Unless you want it for your folks?"

"No, thank you. We made enough Christmas cookies to pave Main Street." She smiled at Abigail. "But that Yule log was amazing.

Next year I'll tell my mom to cut back on the cookies so we can have one."

"That would be great. People did take to it. Two coffees, then?"

"Just coffee is fine for me," Hayley said. "With cream, please."

"Got it. Ryker?"

"Black coffee for me, please, and I'll take a piece of that pumpkin pie with whipped cream." He looked over at Hayley. "Sure you won't change your mind? I'm sure it's good pie."

"I'm sure it is, too. All right. Thank you." She was still adjusting to the disorienting news that Badger had left town. Instead of hanging out at the ranch, he was clear across the country. The distance shouldn't matter because she didn't plan to see him, anyway, but it did. He was too far away and she wanted to ask when he'd be back. No, better not.

Ryker waited until Abigail left before putting a wrapped package in the middle of the table along with a thick envelope. "I promised Badger I'd give you these. But you don't have to take them. No obligation."

Her chest tightened. He'd bought her something for Christmas. It looked like a book. No telling what might be in the envelope, though. "I'll take them." She picked up the package and the envelope and tucked them next to her purse. "Thank you."

"I could have just dropped them by your house, but I...wanted to have a chat, put in a good word for Badger."

"Before we get into that, I owe you an apology. You weren't in favor of our plan and I'm sure it interfered with the visit you'd been looking forward to. I'm sorry for any inconvenience or awkwardness I caused you."

He gazed at her quietly for a moment. "I did think it was a mistake. But turns out it wasn't. Getting involved with you made Badger come to grips with a few things he's been sweeping under the rug."

"Like what?"

"It's all in the letter."

"That thick envelope is a *letter*?"

"Yes, ma'am. Took him three days to write it. He was finishing up when I drove him to the airport first thing this morning."

"I can't remember the last time someone's written me a letter, let alone a long one."

"There's a lot in there. This might sound corny, but it was a labor of love."

She gulped. How should she respond to that? "Why did he...I mean, what gave him the idea?"

"Well, I put the thought in his head, but he did the heavy lifting. See, letters are a big deal when you're in the service. Video chats are great and email is wonderful, too. But there's nothing like an actual letter. You can take it with you and read it wherever you are. No batteries, no electricity required. And it's private."

"But it sounds like you know what's in this one."

"I know in general what he planned to say, because we talked about it. But I haven't read a word of it. That's between Badger and you."

She glanced at the thick envelope sitting next to her chair like a time bomb. She could almost hear it ticking.

"You don't have to stay for the pie and coffee if you need to get home."

She couldn't wait to tear into that letter, but she'd also been given an opportunity to talk privately with Ryker. That could be valuable. "I'd like to stay for pie and coffee. I want to hear more about Badger."

Two hours later, he'd told her some silly stories that made her laugh, like the time Badger had walked all the way to the mess hall on his hands. Then there were the incidents that made her stomach clench. Evidently Badger had developed the habit of ignoring his own safety whenever he'd decided his flying skills could protect his buddies. Several pilots, including Ryker, owed their lives to Badger's bravery.

Outside the diner she gave Ryker a hug and thanked him for being the messenger. Then she hurried home. No one else was there, which gave her the freedom to close herself in her room with the package and the precious envelope.

She opened the package first. She suspected that once she opened the envelope, she'd forget a package even existed.

When she took off the cheerful Christmas wrap, she gasped. Was he psychic? How had he known that she'd coveted this when she'd gone into the collectible shop a week ago? Then again, if he'd asked the owner, she might have remembered.

He must have been eager for her to open it on Christmas Day. And then... She closed her eyes as regret washed over her, leaving behind a hollow ache of longing. Atlanta was too damn far away.

Carefully turning the pages, she gazed at illustrations she'd loved as a child. Her copy of this book, which hadn't been nearly this valuable, had been ruined when she'd left her bedroom window open during a rainstorm. Now she had the book again.

She vowed that at the very least, she'd find a way to thank him. He certainly deserved that.

Laying the book down gently, she opened the envelope and unfolded the sheaf of pages. They were covered with carefully printed words in all caps.

DEAREST HAYLEY,

THANK GOD FOR RYKER, WHO POINTED OUT THAT ALTHOUGH I HAD EVERY REASON TO FALL IN LOVE WITH YOU BECAUSE YOU WERE AN OPEN BOOK, I GAVE YOU NO REASON TO FALL IN LOVE WITH ME BECAUSE I WAS A CLOSED BOOK.

She put down the letter, heart pounding. He'd fallen in love with her? Taking a deep breath, she read on.

THESE PAGES ARE MY POOR ATTEMPT TO TELL YOU EVERYTHING I CAN THINK OF THAT YOU MIGHT WANT TO KNOW. LIKE THE

FACT I HATED MY PARENTS' TV BAN. THE TUTOR
WASN'T MUCH FUN, EITHER.

THIS IS PROBABLY A BORING READ. I
DON'T PRETEND TO BE A GREAT WRITER. AND I
CAN'T IMAGINE THAT YOU'LL BE IN LOVE WITH
ME BY THE END OF IT, IF YOU EVEN MAKE IT
THAT FAR WITHOUT FALLING ASLEEP.

BUT IF YOU SHOULD MANAGE TO WADE
THROUGH IT, AT LEAST YOU'LL HAVE A BETTER
IDEA OF WHO I AM. MOSTLY I'M A GUY WHO'S
DESPERATELY IN LOVE WITH YOU.

FOREVER YOURS,

*Thaddeus Livingston Calhoun III, aka
Badger*

P.S. I'LL BE IN OUR ROOM AT THE B&B
ON NEW YEAR'S EVE WITH A BOTTLE OF
CHAMPAGNE AND HOPE IN MY HEART.

* * *

Badger paced the confines of the room,
which had seemed plenty big enough a week ago
and had shrunk drastically since then. Mrs.
Stanislowski had provided an ice bucket, ice and
two champagne glasses. She'd also given him a
hug and wished him luck. He surely could use it.

Writing the letter to Hayley had been a
catharsis he'd needed for a long time. Going
through his things at his childhood home in
Buckhead would have been far more painful if he
hadn't written it. He'd walked out of that house
with no regrets about the decision he'd made to
leave Atlanta for good.

But if Hayley didn't show up tonight...

He'd taken chances all his life. He'd driven too fast, partied too hard and flown the F-15 like a crazy person.

Yet he'd never feared the outcome of any risky move more than he did this one. He'd gutted himself in the letter, allowing her to see the good, the bad and the ugly. No one else, not even his parents or Ryker, knew all the things he'd put in there.

The clock downstairs had struck the half-hour about ten minutes ago. He'd left the door open so he could hear if someone started up the stairs. Every time it happened, he broke out in a sweat.

A small party was going on in the breakfast room and people were coming and going because of it. They would climb up the first flight, he'd hold his breath, and they'd proceed down the hallway while he sucked in air.

This was hell. What had he been thinking? But he'd put it in the letter and he had to follow through. Why hadn't he just said *call me* at the bottom instead of setting up this stupid-ass dramatic meeting? Why hadn't he—okay, another person was on the stairs.

By now he could count the steps. Nine, ten, eleven, twelve. Whoever it was, they'd reached the first landing. In a second, they'd walk down the hall and he could breathe again. But they didn't walk down the hall. They started up the second flight.

Hayley? Or someone who'd had too much champagne and was lost? If it was Hayley, he didn't want her to see him turning blue from lack of air.

Forcing himself to breathe, he lost count of the steps. Then he glanced around. If it was her, he should appear relaxed and casual. He pulled out one of the two chairs at the table and sat facing the door. Yeah, that was casual, all right, sitting bolt upright and staring at the…

Hayley appeared in the doorway. She looked just as scared as he was. Her parka was unzipped and she clutched her purse to her chest. She wasn't wearing the ring.

He stood. Swallowed. Couldn't come up with a single thing to say.

She took a shaky breath. "Happy New Year."

"Same to you." *Brilliant, Calhoun.*

"Thank you for the book. I love it."

"Good. I'm glad." His heart was beating way too fast.

She gazed at him in silence before taking another deep breath.

"Did you really pee in the fountain at your folks' house?"

"Yes." His voice sounded rusty. He cleared his throat. "You read my letter?"

"Every word." She was shaking. "I read it three times."

"Three?"

"Yes." She clutched her purse tighter. "The first page, more than three. A bunch."

"I meant what I wrote." Now he was shaking, too. "I love you, Hayley."

"I know." She took a step forward. "Badger, I—"

"One letter isn't enough. I'm aware of that." He drifted a little closer. How he'd missed her sapphire blue eyes.

"About that letter." She loosened her hold on her purse and it fell to the floor with a soft thud. "Ryker said it took you three days." She was close, now, real close.

He breathed in the scent of her perfume. "I put in as much as I could because I'm hopin' that someday, after we've spent more time together, you'll begin to love me back."

She flattened her palms against his chest. "Someday?" She didn't look scared anymore.

The warmth of her hands after all this time gave him a jolt of such intense pleasure that he gasped. Did he dare hope? "Believe me, I'm not expectin'—"

Her sweet lips ended that sentence.

With a groan, he wrapped his arms around her, parka and all. Lord have mercy, he was kissing Hayley again. And even better, she was kissing him. Like she meant it. Like she wanted to keep on doing it.

But eventually she did ease away and the light in her eyes was breathtaking. "What if I already love you back?"

His ears buzzed as he stared at her in disbelief. Had he heard that right?

"You're amazing. You're brave and funny and sweet and full of the devil, too." Her warm gaze held his. "I love you, Thaddeus Livingston Calhoun the Third. I love you back."

He gulped. "Well, hallelujah and pass the black-eyed peas."

She laughed.

He did, too. Joy. So much joy. More than a body had a right to. But he'd take it and be forever grateful.

"There's that grin I've been missing."

"You missed my grin?"

"I've missed every single thing about you." She wound her arms around his neck. "That's one of the reasons I'm moving to Eagles Nest."

"You are?" The happiness just kept piling up on him.

"I have a few things to work out, but I've made my decision. I don't want to have to miss you anymore, Badger."

"You won't have to." Lowering his head, he brushed her lips with his. "Not if I can help it."

"And by the way, the ring's in my purse."

"Oh?" He lifted his head.

"I'm giving it back to you." She said it with the sweetest smile.

"You don't want it?"

"Oh, I do, but not yet. First we need to learn more about each other. And then, when the time is right, you can propose for real. Or maybe I'll propose to you."

"How will we know when the time is right?"

"That's why we need to learn about each other. So we'll know."

"This is goin' to be one excitin' journey. I can't wait to get started." Leaning down, he touched his mouth to hers just as the folks downstairs began blowing horns and making noise.

She drew back and gazed up at him. "Happy New Year, Badger."

"Happy New Year, darlin'."

"It's going to be a great year."

"Yes, ma'am." Oh, yeah, it would be the best ever. Hayley would be in it. With a sigh of pleasure, he claimed his first kiss of the New Year, the first of many, many more.

Valentine's Day is all about romance, and Luke Bennett can't imagine anything sweeter than sharing a valentine kiss with Pie in the Sky Bakery owner Abigail Summers in A COWBOY'S KISS, book seven in the McGavin Brothers series!

* * * * *

"I'm Luke Bennett, by the way."

"Abigail Summers." She held out her hand. "I own the—"

"Pie in the Sky Bakery." He clasped her hand. Her grip was firm, probably from kneading dough. "I was trying to remember where I'd heard your name. I've only been in once with my folks over Christmas vacation to pick up a few breakfast pastries. I don't remember seeing you."

"I was probably delivering pies and bread to the GG. That was a super busy time."

"I'll bet."

"Am I right that you've just relocated from Portland? I seem to remember your mom saying something like that."

He went on alert. His mom was a recovering matchmaker who'd vowed to mend her ways. But if she'd been talking him up to Abigail, then she might have fallen off the wagon. "Did she happen to mention that I'm single?"

"No." She looked amused. "Was she supposed to?"

"No! I just—"

"Wanted me to know you're available?"

"Absolutely not." Heat rose from under his collar. "That came out all wrong. I'm not in the market."

"You already have a girlfriend?"

"No, I don't, but—"

"You're looking for a boyfriend?"

"*No.*" He scrubbed a hand over his face. Could this get any worse? His mom had kept her word about not trying to set him up. Explaining her previous irritating behavior to Abigail would get him out of this fix but it wouldn't be gallant.

A bump against his thigh made him glance down. Saved by the dog. The collie stood staring up at him as if he, or *she,* needed something.

Abigail chuckled. "That look means *I need to go outside.*"

He met her calm gaze. Too bad he was still embarrassed as hell. And now they were discussing the dog's bathroom requirements. "How do you know?"

"My family had dogs when I was growing up. That's the look they give you when they need to take care of business." The corners of her mouth tilted up. "And then you'll know if it's a boy or a girl."

"I don't have a collar and leash for her."

Opening her coat, she unwound a long scarf from around her neck. "Use this."

"I don't think—"

"Use it." She shook it at him. "Tomorrow you can buy what you need. Today you need to improvise."

She was right. "Thank you, ma'am."

"You're welcome."

The scarf worked like a charm. He secured it around the dog's neck and led the critter back out the front door and over to an area beside the parking lot. As the dog squatted to relieve herself, he had his answer. He'd rescued a girl.

New York Times bestselling author Vicki Lewis Thompson's love affair with cowboys started with the Lone Ranger, continued through Maverick, and took a turn south of the border with Zorro. She views cowboys as the Western version of knights in shining armor, rugged men who value honor, honesty and hard work. Fortunately for her, she lives in the Arizona desert, where broad-shouldered, lean-hipped cowboys abound. Blessed with such an abundance of inspiration, she only hopes that she can do them justice.

For more information about this prolific author, visit her website and sign up for her newsletter. She loves connecting with readers.

VickiLewisThompson.com